I0567232

W.W. JACOBS – THE SHORT STORIES
VOLUME 4

William Wymark Jacobs was born on September 8th, 1863 in the Wapping district of London, England. Jacobs grew up near the docks, where his father was a wharf manager. The docks and river side would be a constant theme of his writing in years to come.

Although surrounded by poverty, he received a formal education in London, first at a private prep school and later at the Birkbeck Literary and Scientific Institute.

His working life began with a less than exciting clerical position at the Post Office Savings Bank. Jacobs put his imagination to good use writing short stories, sketches and articles, many for the Post Office house publication "Blackfriars Magazine."

In 1896 Jacobs published Many Cargoes, a selection of sea-faring yarns, which established him as a popular writer with a knack for authentic dialogue and trick endings.

A year later he published a novelette, The Skipper's Wooing, and in 1898 another collection of short stories; Sea Urchins. These works painted vivid pictures of dockland and seafaring London full of colourful characters.

By 1899, Jacobs was able to quit the post office and write full-time.

He married the noted suffragist Agnes Eleanor Williams (who had been jailed for her protest activities) in 1900. They set up households both in Loughton, Essex and in central London.

The publication in 1902 of At Sunwich Port and Dialstone Lane, in 1904, cemented Jacobs' reputation as one of the leading British authors of the new century.

There followed a string of further successful publications, including Captain's All (1905), Night Watches (1914), The Castaways (1916), and Sea Whispers (1926).

Though Jacobs would create little in the way of new work after 1911, he still wrote and was recognized as a leading humorist, ranked alongside such writers as P. G. Wodehouse.

William Wymark Jacobs died in a North London nursing home in Hornsey Lane, Islington on September 1st, 1943.

Index of Contents

CAPTAIN ROGERS

A man came slowly over the old stone bridge, and averting his gaze from the dark river with its silent craft, looked with some satisfaction toward the feeble lights of the small town on the other side. He walked with the painful, forced step of one who has already trudged far. His worsted hose, where they were not darned, were in holes, and his coat and knee-breeches were rusty with much wear, but he straightened himself as he reached the end of the bridge and stepped out bravely to the taverns which stood in a row facing the quay.

He passed the "Queen Anne"—a mere beershop—without pausing, and after a glance apiece at the "Royal George" and the "Trusty Anchor," kept on his way to where the "Golden Key" hung out a gilded emblem. It was the best house in Riverstone, and patronized by the gentry, but he adjusted his faded coat, and with a swaggering air entered and walked boldly into the coffee-room.

The room was empty, but a bright fire afforded a pleasant change to the chill October air outside. He drew up a chair, and placing his feet on the fender, exposed his tattered soles to the blaze, as a waiter who had just seen him enter the room came and stood aggressively inside the door.

"Brandy and water," said the stranger; "hot."

"The coffee-room is for gentlemen staying in the house," said the waiter.

The stranger took his feet from the fender, and rising slowly, walked toward him. He was a short man and thin, but there was something so menacing in his attitude, and something so fearsome in his stony brown eyes, that the other, despite his disgust for ill-dressed people, moved back uneasily.

"Brandy and water, hot," repeated the stranger; "and plenty of it. D'ye hear?"

The man turned slowly to depart.

"Stop!" said the other, imperiously. "What's the name of the landlord here?"

"Mullet," said the fellow, sulkily.

"Send him to me," said the other, resuming his seat; "and hark you, my friend, more civility, or 'twill be the worse for you."

He stirred the log on the fire with his foot until a shower of sparks whirled up the chimney. The door opened, and the landlord, with the waiter behind him, entered the room, but he still gazed placidly at the glowing embers.

"What do you want?" demanded the landlord, in a deep voice.

The stranger turned a little weazened yellow face and grinned at him familiarly.

"Send that fat rascal of yours away," he said, slowly.

The landlord started at his voice and eyed him closely; then he signed to the man to withdraw, and closing the door behind him, stood silently watching his visitor.

"You didn't expect to see me, Rogers," said the latter.

"My name's Mullet," said the other, sternly. "What do you want?"

"Oh, Mullet?" said the other, in surprise. "I'm afraid I've made a mistake, then. I thought you were my old shipmate, Captain Rogers. It's a foolish mistake of mine, as I've no doubt Rogers was hanged years ago. You never had a brother named Rogers, did you?"

"I say again, what do you want?" demanded the other, advancing upon him.

"Since you're so good," said the other. "I want new clothes, food, and lodging of the best, and my pockets filled with money."

"You had better go and look for all those things, then," said Mullet. "You won't find them here."

"Ay!" said the other, rising. "Well, well—There was a hundred guineas on the head of my old shipmate Rogers some fifteen years ago. I'll see whether it has been earned yet."

"If I gave you a hundred guineas," said the innkeeper, repressing his passion by a mighty effort, "you would not be satisfied."

"Reads like a book," said the stranger, in tones of pretended delight. "What a man it is!"

He fell back as he spoke, and thrusting his hand into his pocket, drew forth a long pistol as the innkeeper, a man of huge frame, edged toward him.

"Keep your distance," he said, in a sharp, quick voice.

The innkeeper, in no wise disturbed at the pistol, turned away calmly, and ringing the bell, ordered some spirits. Then taking a chair, he motioned to the other to do the same, and they sat in silence until the staring waiter had left the room again. The stranger raised his glass.

"My old friend Captain Rogers," he said, solemnly, "and may he never get his deserts!"

"From what jail have you come?" inquired Mullet, sternly.

"'Pon my soul," said the other, "I have been in so many—looking for Captain Rogers—that I almost forget the last, but I have just tramped from London, two hundred and eighty odd miles, for the pleasure of seeing your damned ugly figure-head again; and now I've found it, I'm going to stay. Give me some money."

The innkeeper, without a word, drew a little gold and silver from his pocket, and placing it on the table, pushed it toward him.

"Enough to go on with," said the other, pocketing it; "in future it is halves. D'ye hear me? Halves! And I'll stay here and see I get it."

He sat back in his chair, and meeting the other's hatred with a gaze as steady as his own, replaced his pistol.

"A nice snug harbor after our many voyages," he continued. "Shipmates we were, shipmates we'll be; while Nick Gunn is alive you shall never want for company. Lord! Do you remember the Dutch brig, and the fat frightened mate?"

"I have forgotten it," said the other, still eyeing him steadfastly. "I have forgotten many things. For fifteen years I have lived a decent, honest life. Pray God for your own sinful soul, that the devil in me does not wake again."

"Fifteen years is a long nap," said Gunn, carelessly; "what a godsend it 'll be for you to have me by you to remind you of old times! Why, you're looking smug, man; the honest innkeeper to the life! Gad! who's the girl?"

He rose and made a clumsy bow as a girl of eighteen, after a moment's hesitation at the door, crossed over to the innkeeper.

"I'm busy, my dear," said the latter, somewhat sternly.

"Our business," said Gunn, with another bow, "is finished. Is this your daughter, Rog— Mullet?"

"My stepdaughter," was the reply.

Gunn placed a hand, which lacked two fingers, on his breast, and bowed again.

"One of your father's oldest friends," he said smoothly; "and fallen on evil days; I'm sure your gentle heart will be pleased to hear that your good father has requested me—for a time—to make his house my home."

"Any friend of my father's is welcome to me, sir," said the girl, coldly. She looked from the innkeeper to his odd-looking guest, and conscious of something strained in the air, gave him a little bow and quitted the room.

"You insist upon staying, then?" said Mullet, after a pause.

"More than ever," replied Gunn, with a leer toward the door. "Why, you don't think I'm *afraid*, Captain? You should know me better than that."

"Life is sweet," said the other.

"Ay," assented Gunn, "so sweet that you will share things with me to keep it."

"No," said the other, with great calm. "I am man enough to have a better reason."

"No psalm singing," said Gunn, coarsely. "And look cheerful, you old buccaneer. Look as a man should look who has just met an old friend never to lose him again."

He eyed his man expectantly and put his hand to his pocket again, but the innkeeper's face was troubled, and he gazed stolidly at the fire.

"See what fifteen years' honest, decent life does for us," grinned the intruder.

The other made no reply, but rising slowly, walked to the door without a word.

"Landlord," cried Gunn, bringing his maimed hand sharply down on the table.

The innkeeper turned and regarded him.

"Send me in some supper," said Gunn; "the best you have, and plenty of it, and have a room prepared. The best."

The door closed silently, and was opened a little later by the dubious George coming in to set a bountiful repast. Gunn, after cursing him for his slowness and awkwardness, drew his chair to the table and made the meal of one seldom able to satisfy his hunger. He finished at last, and after sitting for some time smoking, with his legs sprawled on the fender, rang for a candle and demanded to be shown to his room.

His proceedings when he entered it were but a poor compliment to his host. Not until he had poked and pried into every corner did he close the door. Then, not content with locking it, he tilted a chair beneath the handle, and placing his pistol beneath his pillow, fell fast asleep.

Despite his fatigue he was early astir next morning. Breakfast was laid for him in the coffee-room, and his brow darkened. He walked into the hall, and after trying various doors entered a small sitting-room, where his host and daughter sat at breakfast, and with an easy assurance drew a chair to the table. The innkeeper helped him without a word, but the girl's hand shook under his gaze as she passed him some coffee.

"As soft a bed as ever I slept in," he remarked.

"I hope that you slept well," said the girl, civilly.

"Like a child," said Gunn, gravely; "an easy conscience. Eh, Mullet?"

The innkeeper nodded and went on eating. The other, after another remark or two, followed his example, glancing occasionally with warm approval at the beauty of the girl who sat at the head of the table.

"A sweet girl," he remarked, as she withdrew at the end of the meal; "and no mother, I presume?"

"No mother," repeated the other.

Gunn sighed and shook his head.

"A sad case, truly," he murmured. "No mother and such a guardian. Poor soul, if she but knew! Well, we must find her a husband."

He looked down as he spoke, and catching sight of his rusty clothes and broken shoes, clapped his hand to his pocket; and with a glance at his host, sallied out to renew his wardrobe. The innkeeper, with an inscrutable face, watched him down the quay, then with bent head he returned to the house and fell to work on his accounts.

In this work Gunn, returning an hour later, clad from head to foot in new apparel, offered to assist him. Mullett hesitated, but made no demur; neither did he join in the ecstasies which his new partner displayed at the sight of the profits. Gunn put some more gold into his new pockets, and throwing himself back in a chair, called loudly to George to bring him some drink.

In less than a month the intruder was the virtual master of the "Golden Key." Resistance on the part of the legitimate owner became more and more feeble, the slightest objection on his part drawing from the truculent Gunn dark allusions to his past and threats against his future, which for the sake of his daughter he could not ignore. His health began to fail, and Joan watched with perplexed terror the growth of a situation which was in a fair way of becoming unbearable.

The arrogance of Gunn knew no bounds. The maids learned to tremble at his polite grin, or his worse freedom, and the men shrank appalled from his profane wrath. George, after ten years' service, was brutally dismissed, and refusing to accept dismissal from his hands, appealed to his master. The innkeeper confirmed it, and with lack-lustre eyes fenced feebly when his daughter, regardless of Gunn's presence, indignantly appealed to him.

"The man was rude to my friend, my dear," he said dispiritedly

"If he was rude, it was because Mr. Gunn deserved it," said Joan, hotly.

Gunn laughed uproariously.

"Gad, my dear, I like you!" he cried, slapping his leg. "You're a girl of spirit. Now I will make you a fair offer. If you ask for George to stay, stay he shall, as a favour to your sweet self."

The girl trembled.

"Who is master here?" she demanded, turning a full eye on her father.

Mullet laughed uneasily.

"This is business," he said, trying to speak lightly, "and women can't understand it. Gunn is—is valuable to me, and George must go."

"Unless you plead for him, sweet one?" said Gunn.

The girl looked at her father again, but he turned his head away and tapped on the floor with his foot. Then in perplexity, akin to tears, she walked from the room, carefully drawing her dress aside as Gunn held the door for her.

"A fine girl," said Gunn, his thin lips working; "a fine spirit. 'Twill be pleasant to break it; but she does not know who is master here."

"She is young yet," said the other, hurriedly.

"I will soon age her if she looks like that at me again," said Gunn. "By —, I'll turn out the whole crew into the street, and her with them, an' I wish it. I'll lie in my bed warm o' nights and think of her huddled on a doorstep."

His voice rose and his fists clenched, but he kept his distance and watched the other warily. The innkeeper's face was contorted and his brow grew wet. For one moment something peeped out of his eyes; the next he sat down in his chair again and nervously fingered his chin.

"I have but to speak," said Gunn, regarding him with much satisfaction, "and you will hang, and your money go to the Crown. What will become of her then, think you?"

The other laughed nervously.

"'Twould be stopping the golden eggs," he ventured.

"Don't think too much of that," said Gunn, in a hard voice. "I was never one to be baulked, as you know."

"Come, come. Let us be friends," said Mullet; "the girl is young, and has had her way."

He looked almost pleadingly at the other, and his voice trembled. Gunn drew himself up, and regarding him with a satisfied sneer, quitted the room without a word.

Affairs at the "Golden Key" grew steadily worse and worse. Gunn dominated the place, and his vile personality hung over it like a shadow. Appeals to the innkeeper were in vain; his health was breaking fast, and he moodily declined to interfere. Gunn appointed servants of his own choosing-brazen maids and foul-mouthed men. The old patrons ceased to frequent the "Golden Key," and its bedrooms stood empty. The maids scarcely deigned to take an order from Joan, and the men spoke to her familiarly. In the midst of all this the innkeeper, who had complained once or twice of vertigo, was seized with a fit.

Joan, flying to him for protection against the brutal advances of Gunn, found him lying in a heap behind the door of his small office, and in her fear called loudly for assistance. A little knot of servants collected, and stood regarding him stupidly. One made a brutal jest. Gunn, pressing through the throng, turned the senseless body over with his foot, and cursing vilely, ordered them to carry it upstairs.

Until the surgeon came, Joan, kneeling by the bed, held on to the senseless hand as her only protection against the evil faces of Gunn and his proteges. Gunn himself was taken aback, the innkeeper's death at that time by no means suiting his aims.

The surgeon was a man of few words and fewer attainments, but under his ministrations the innkeeper, after a long interval, rallied. The half-closed eyes opened, and he looked in a dazed fashion at his surroundings. Gunn drove the servants away and questioned the man of medicine. The answers were vague and interspersed with Latin. Freedom from noise and troubles of all kinds was insisted upon and Joan was installed as nurse, with a promise of speedy assistance.

The assistance arrived late in the day in the shape of an elderly woman, whose Spartan treatment of her patients had helped many along the silent road. She commenced her reign by punching the sick man's pillows, and having shaken him into consciousness by this means, gave him a dose of physic, after first tasting it herself from the bottle.

After the first rally the innkeeper began to fail slowly. It was seldom that he understood what was said to him, and pitiful to the beholder to see in his intervals of consciousness his timid anxiety to earn the good-will of the all-powerful Gunn. His strength declined until assistance was needed to turn him in the bed, and his great sinewy hands were forever trembling and fidgeting on the coverlet.

Joan, pale with grief and fear, tended him assiduously. Her stepfather's strength had been a proverb in the town, and many a hasty citizen had felt the strength of his arm. The increasing lawlessness of the house filled her with dismay, and the coarse attentions of Gunn became more persistent than ever. She took her meals in the sick-room, and divided her time between that and her own.

Gunn himself was in a dilemma. With Mullet dead, his power was at an end and his visions of wealth dissipated. He resolved to feather his nest immediately, and interviewed the surgeon. The surgeon was ominously reticent, the nurse cheerfully ghoulish.

"Four days I give him," she said, calmly; "four blessed days, not but what he might slip away at any moment."

Gunn let one day of the four pass, and then, choosing a time when Joan was from the room, entered it for a little quiet conversation. The innkeeper's eyes were open, and, what was more to the purpose, intelligent.

"You're cheating the hangman, after all," snarled Gunn. "I'm off to swear an information."

The other, by a great effort, turned his heavy head and fixed his wistful eyes on him.

"Mercy!" he whispered. "For her sake—give me—a little time!"

"To slip your cable, I suppose," quoth Gunn. "Where's your money? Where's your hoard, you miser?"

Mullet closed his eyes. He opened them again slowly and strove to think, while Gunn watched him narrowly. When he spoke, his utterance was thick and labored.

"Come to-night," he muttered, slowly. "Give me—time—I will make your —your fortune. But the nurse-watches."

"I'll see to her," said Gunn, with a grin. "But tell me now, lest you die first."

"You will—let Joan—have a share?" panted the innkeeper.

"Yes, yes," said Gunn, hastily.

The innkeeper strove to raise himself in the bed, and then fell back again exhausted as Joan's step was heard on the stairs. Gunn gave a savage glance of warning at him, and barring the progress of the girl at the door, attempted to salute her. Joan came in pale and trembling, and falling on her knees by the bedside, took her father's hand in hers and wept over it. The innkeeper gave a faint groan and a shiver ran through his body.

It was nearly an hour after midnight that Nick Gunn, kicking off his shoes, went stealthily out onto the lancing. A little light came from the partly open door of the sick-room, but all else was in blackness. He moved along and peered in.

The nurse was siting in a high-backed oak chair by the fire. She had slipped down in the seat, and her untidy head hung on her bosom. A glass stood on the small oak table by her side, and a solitary candle on the high mantel-piece diffused a sickly light. Gunn entered the room, and finding that the sick man was dozing, shook him roughly.

The innkeeper opened his eyes and gazed at him blankly.

"Wake, you fool," said Gunn, shaking him again.

The other roused and muttered something incoherently. Then he stirred slightly.

"The nurse," he whispered.

"She's safe enow," said Gunn. "I've seen to that."

He crossed the room lightly, and standing before the unconscious woman, inspected her closely and raised her in the chair. Her head fell limply over the arm.

"Dead?" inquired Mullet, in a fearful whisper.

"Drugged," said Gunn, shortly. "Now speak up, and be lively."

The innkeeper's eyes again travelled in the direction of the nurse.

"The man," he whispered; "the servants."

"Dead drunk and asleep," said Gunn, biting the words. "The last day would hardly rouse them. Now will you speak, damn you!"

"I must—take care—of Joan," said the father.

Gunn shook his clenched hand at him.

"My money—is—is—" said the other. "Promise me on—your oath—Joan."

"Ay, ay." growled Gunn; "how many more times? I'll marry her, and she shall have what I choose to give her. Speak up, you fool! It's not for you to make terms. Where is it?"

He bent over, but Mullet, exhausted with his efforts, had closed his eyes again, and half turned his head.

"Where is it, damn you?" said Gunn, from between his teeth.

Mullet opened his eyes again, glanced fearfully round the room, and whispered. Gunn, with a stifled oath, bent his ear almost to his mouth, and the next moment his neck was in the grip of the strongest man in Riverstone, and an arm like a bar of iron over his back pinned him down across the bed.

"You dog!" hissed a fierce voice in his ear. "I've got you—Captain Rogers at your service, and now you may tell his name to all you can. Shout it, you spawn of hell. Shout it!"

He rose in bed, and with a sudden movement flung the other over on his back. Gunn's eyes were starting from his head, and he writhed convulsively.

"I thought you were a sharper man, Gunn," said Rogers, still in the same hot whisper, as he relaxed his grip a little; "you are too simple, you hound! When you first threatened me I resolved to kill you. Then you threatened my daughter. I wish that you had nine lives, that I might take them all. Keep still!"

He gave a half-glance over his shoulder at the silent figure of the nurse, and put his weight on the twisting figure on the bed.

"You drugged the hag, good Gunn," he continued. "To-morrow morning, Gunn, they will find you in your room dead, and if one of the scum you brought into my house be charged with the murder, so much the better. When I am well they will go. I am already feeling a little bit stronger, Gunn, as you see, and in a month I hope to be about again."

He averted his face, and for a time gazed sternly and watchfully at the door. Then he rose slowly to his feet, and taking the dead man in his arms, bore him slowly and carefully to his room, and laid him a huddled heap on the floor. Swiftly and noiselessly he put the dead man's shoes on and turned his pockets inside out, kicked a rug out of place, and put a guinea on the floor. Then he stole cautiously down stairs and set a small door at the back open. A dog barked frantically, and he hurried back to his room. The nurse still slumbered by the fire.

She awoke in the morning shivering with the cold, and being jealous of her reputation, rekindled the fire, and measuring out the dose which the invalid should have taken, threw it away. On these unconscious preparations for an alibi Captain Rogers gazed through half-closed lids, and then turning his grim face to the wall, waited for the inevitable alarm.

THE CAPTAIN'S EXPLOIT

It was a wet, dreary night in that cheerless part of the great metropolis known as Wapping. The rain, which had been falling heavily for hours, still fell steadily on to the sloppy pavements and roads, and joining forces in the gutter, rushed impetuously to the nearest sewer.

The two or three streets which had wedged themselves in between the docks and the river, and which, as a matter of fact, really comprise the beginning and end of Wapping, were deserted, except for a belated van crashing over the granite roads, or the chance form of a dock-labourer plodding doggedly along, with head bent in distaste for the rain, and hands sunk in trouser-pockets.

"Beastly night," said Captain Bing, as he rolled out of the private bar of the "Sailor's Friend," and, ignoring the presence of the step, took a little hurried run across the pavement. "Not fit for a dog to be out in."

He kicked, as he spoke, at a shivering cur which was looking in at the crack of the bar-door, with a hazy view of calling its attention to the matter, and then, pulling up the collar of his rough pea-jacket, stepped boldly out into the rain. Three or four minutes' walk, or rather roll, brought him to a dark narrow passage, which ran between two houses to the water-side. By a slight tack to starboard at a critical moment he struck the channel safely, and followed it until it ended in a flight of old stone steps, half of which were under water.

"Where for?" inquired a man, starting up from a small penthouse formed of rough pieces of board.

"Schooner in the tier, Smiling Jane," said the captain gruffly, as he stumbled clumsily into a boat and sat down in the stern. "Why don't you have better seats in this 'ere boat?"

"They're there, if you'll look for them," said the waterman; "and you'll find 'em easier sitting than that bucket."

"Why don't you put 'em where a man can see 'em?" inquired the captain, raising his voice a little.

The other opened his mouth to reply, but realising that it would lead to a long and utterly futile argument, contented himself with asking his fare to trim the boat better; and, pushing off from the steps, pulled strongly through the dark lumpy water. The tide was strong, so that they made but slow progress.

"When I was a young man," said the fare with severity, "I'd ha' pulled this boat across and back afore now."

"When you was a young man," said the man at the oars, who had a local reputation as a wit, "there wasn't no boats; they was all Noah's arks then."

"Stow your gab," said the captain, after a pause of deep thought.

The other, whose besetting sin was certainly not loquacity, ejected a thin stream of tobacco-juice over the side, spat on his hands, and continued his laborious work until a crowd of dark shapes, surmounted by a network of rigging, loomed up before them.

"Now, which is your little barge?" he inquired, tugging strongly to maintain his position against the fast-flowing tide.

"Smiling Jane" said his fare.

"Ah," said the waterman, "Smiling Jane, is it? You sit there, cap'n, an' I'll row round all their sterns while you strike matches and look at the names. We'll have quite a nice little evening."

"There she is," cried the captain, who was too muddled to notice the sarcasm; "there's the little beauty. Steady, my lad."

He reached out his hand as he spoke, and as the boat jarred violently against a small schooner, seized a rope which hung over the side, and, swaying to and fro, fumbled in his pocket for the fare.

"Steady, old boy," said the waterman affectionately. He had just received twopence-halfpenny and a shilling by mistake for threepence.

"Easy up the side. You ain't such a pretty figger as you was when your old woman made such a bad bargain."

The captain paused in his climb, and poising himself on one foot, gingerly felt for his tormentor's head with the other Not finding it, he flung his leg over the bulwark, and gained the deck of the vessel as the boat swung round with the tide and disappeared in the darkness.

"All turned in," said the captain, gazing owlishly at the deserted deck. "Well, there's a good hour an' a half afore we start; I'll turn in too."

He walked slowly aft, and sliding back the companion-hatch, descended into a small evil-smelling cabin, and stood feeling in the darkness for the matches. They were not to be found, and, growling profanely, he felt his way to the state-room, and turned in all standing.

It was still dark when he awoke, and hanging over the edge of the bunk, cautiously felt for the floor with his feet, and having found it, stood thoughtfully scratching his head, which seemed to have swollen to abnormal proportions.

"Time they were getting under weigh," he said at length, and groping his way to the foot of the steps, he opened the door of what looked like a small pantry, but which was really the mate's boudoir.

"Jem," said the captain gruffly.

There was no reply, and jumping to the conclusion that he was above, the captain tumbled up the steps and gained the deck, which, as far as he could see, was in the same deserted condition as when he left it.

Anxious to get some idea of the time, he staggered to the side and looked over. The tide was almost at the turn, and the steady clank, clank of neighbouring windlasses showed that other craft were just getting under weigh. A barge, its red light turning the water to blood, with a huge wall of dark sail, passed noiselessly by, the indistinct figure of a man leaning skilfully upon the tiller.

As these various signs of life and activity obtruded themselves upon the skipper of the Smiling Jane, his wrath rose higher and higher as he looked around the wet, deserted deck of his own little craft. Then he walked forward and thrust his head down the forecastle hatchway.

As he expected, there was a complete sleeping chorus below; the deep satisfied snoring of half-a-dozen seamen, who, regardless of the tide and their captain's feelings, were slumbering sweetly, in blissful ignorance of all that the Lancet might say upon the twin subjects of overcrowding and ventilation.

"Below there, you lazy thieves!" roared the captain; "tumble up, tumble up!"

The snores stopped. "Ay, ay!" said a sleepy voice. "What's the matter, master?"

"Matter!" repeated the other, choking violently. "Ain't you going to sail to-night?"

"To-night!" said another voice, in surprise. "Why, I thought we wasn't going to sail till Wen'sday."

Not trusting himself to reply, so careful was he of the morals of his men, the skipper went and leaned over the side and communed with the silent water. In an incredibly short space of time five or six dusky figures pattered up on to the deck, and a minute or two later the harsh clank of the windlass echoed far and wide.

The captain took the wheel. A fat and very sleepy seaman put up the side-lights, and the little schooner, detaching itself by the aid of boat-hooks and fenders from the neighbouring craft, moved slowly down with the tide. The men, in response to the captain's fervent orders, climbed aloft, and sail after sail was spread to the gentle breeze.

"Hi! you there," cried the captain to one of the men who stood near him, coiling up some loose line.

"Sir?" said the man.

"Where is the mate?" inquired the captain.

"Man with red whiskers and pimply nose?" said the man interrogatively.

"That's him to a hair," answered the other.

"Ain't seen him since he took me on at eleven," said the man. "How many new hands are there?"

"I b'leeve we're all fresh," was the reply. "I don't believe some of 'em have ever smelt salt water afore."

"The mate's been at it again," said the captain warmly, "that's what he has. He's done it afore and got left behind. Them what can't stand drink, my man, shouldn't take it, remember that."

"He said we wasn't going to sail till Wen'sday," remarked the man, who found the captain's attitude rather trying.

"He'll get sacked, that's what he'll get," said the captain warmly. "I shall report him as soon as I get ashore."

The subject exhausted, the seaman returned to his work, and the captain continued steering in moody silence.

Slowly, slowly darkness gave way to light. The different portions of the craft, instead of all being blurred into one, took upon themselves shape, and stood out wet and distinct in the cold grey of the breaking day. But the lighter it became, the harder the skipper stared and rubbed his eyes, and looked from the deck to the flat marshy shore, and from the shore back to the deck again.

"Here, come here," he cried, beckoning to one of the crew.

"Yessir," said the man, advancing.

"There's something in one of my eyes," faltered the skipper. "I can't see straight; everything seems mixed up. Now, speaking deliberate and without any hurry, which side o' the ship do you say the cook's galley's on?"

"Starboard," said the man promptly, eyeing him with astonishment.

"Starboard," repeated the other softly. "He says starboard, and that's what it seems to me. My lad, yesterday morning it was on the port side."

The seaman received this astounding communication with calmness, but, as a slight concession to appearances, said "Lor!"

"And the water-cask," said the skipper; "what colour is it?"

"Green," said the man.

"Not white?" inquired the skipper, leaning heavily upon the wheel.

"Whitish-green," said the man, who always believed in keeping in with his superior officers.

The captain swore at him.

By this time two or three of the crew who had over-heard part of the conversation had collected aft, and now stood in a small wondering knot before their strange captain.

"My lads," said the latter, moistening his dry lips with his tongue, "I name no names—I don't know 'em yet—and I cast no suspicions, but somebody has been painting up and altering this 'ere craft, and twisting things about until a man 'ud hardly know her. Now what's the little game"

There was no answer, and the captain, who was seeing things clearer and clearer in the growing light, got paler and paler.

"I must be going crazy," he muttered. "Is this the SMILING JANE, or am I dreaming?"

"It ain't the SMILING JANE," said one of the seamen; "leastways," he added cautiously, "it wasn't when I came aboard."

"Not the SMILING JANE!" roared the skipper; "what is it, then?"

"Why, the MARY ANN," chorused the astonished crew.

"My lads," faltered the agonised captain after a long pause. "My lads—" He stopped and swallowed something in his throat. "I've been and brought away the wrong ship," he continued with an effort; "that's what I've done. I must have been bewitched."

"Well, who's having the little game now?" inquired a voice.

"Somebody else'll be sacked as well as the mate," said another.

"We must take her back," said the captain, raising his voice to drown these mutterings. "Stand by there!"

The bewildered crew went to their posts, the captain gave his orders in a voice which had never been so subdued and mellow since it broke at the age of fourteen, and the Mary Ann took in sail, and, dropping her anchor, waited patiently for the turning of the tide.

The church bells in Wapping and Rotherhithe were just striking the hour of mid-day, though they were heard by few above the noisy din of workers on wharves and ships, as a short stout captain, and a mate with red whiskers and a pimply nose, stood up in a waterman's boat in the centre of the river, and gazed at each other in blank astonishment.

"She's gone, clean gone!" murmured the bewildered captain.

"Clean as a whistle," said the mate. "The new hands must ha' run away with her."

Then the bereaved captain raised his voice, and pronounced a pathetic and beautiful eulogy upon the departed vessel, somewhat marred by an appendix in which he consigned the new hands, their heirs, and descendants, to everlasting perdition.

"Ahoy!" said the waterman, who was getting tired of the business, addressing a grimy-looking seaman hanging meditatively over the side of a schooner. "Where's the Mary Ann?"

"Went away at half-past one this morning," was the reply.

"'Cos here's the cap'n an' the mate," said the waterman, indicating the forlorn couple with a bob of his head.

"My eyes!" said the man, "I s'pose the cook's in charge then. We was to have gone too, but our old man hasn't turned up."

Quickly the news spread amongst the craft in the tier, and many and various were the suggestions shouted to the bewildered couple from the different decks. At last, just as the captain had ordered the waterman to return to the shore, he was startled by a loud cry from the mate.

"Look there!" he shouted.

The captain looked. Fifty or sixty yards away, a small shamefaced-looking schooner, so it appeared to his excited imagination, was slowly approaching them. A minute later a shout went up from the other craft as she took in sail and bore slowly down upon them. Then a small boat put off to the buoy, and the Mary Ann was slowly warped into the place she had left ten hours before.

But while all this was going on, she was boarded by her captain and mate. They were met by Captain Bing, supported by his mate, who had hastily pushed off from the Smiling Jane to the assistance of his chief.

In the two leading features before mentioned he was not unlike the mate of the Mary Ann, and much stress was laid upon this fact by the unfortunate Bing in his explanation. So much so, in fact, that both the mates got restless; the skipper, who was a plain man, and given to calling a spade a spade, using the word "pimply" with what seemed to them unnecessary iteration.

It is possible that the interview might have lasted for hours had not Bing suddenly changed his tactics and begun to throw out dark hints about standing a dinner ashore, and settling it over a friendly glass. The face of the Mary Ann's captain began to clear, and, as Bing proceeded from generalities to details, a soft smile played over his expressive features. It was reflected in the faces of the mates, who by these means showed clearly that they understood the table was to be laid for four.

At this happy turn of affairs Bing himself smiled, and a little while later a ship's boat containing four boon companions put off from the Mary Ann and made for the shore. Of what afterwards ensued there is no distinct record, beyond what may be gleaned from the fact that the quartette turned up at midnight arm-in-arm, and affectionately refused to be separated—even to enter the ship's boat, which was waiting for them. The sailors were at first rather nonplussed, but by dint of much coaxing and argument broke up the party, and rowing them to their respective vessels, put them carefully to bed.

CAPTAINS ALL

Every sailorman grumbles about the sea, said the night-watchman, thoughtfully. It's human nature to grumble, and I s'pose they keep on grumbling and sticking to it because there ain't much else they can do. There's not many shore-going berths that a sailorman is fit for, and those that they are—such as a night-watchman's, for instance—wants such a good character that there's few as are to equal it.

Sometimes they get things to do ashore. I knew one man that took up butchering, and 'e did very well at it till the police took him up. Another man I knew gave up the sea to marry a washerwoman, and they hadn't been married six months afore she died, and back he 'ad to go to sea agin, pore chap.

A man who used to grumble awful about the sea was old Sam Small—a man I've spoke of to you before. To hear 'im go on about the sea, arter he 'ad spent four or five months' money in a fortnight, was 'artbreaking. He used to ask us wot was going to happen to 'im in his old age, and when we pointed out that he wouldn't be likely to 'ave any old age if he wasn't more careful of 'imself he used to fly into a temper and call us everything 'e could lay his tongue to.

One time when 'e was ashore with Peter Russet and Ginger Dick he seemed to 'ave got it on the brain. He started being careful of 'is money instead o' spending it, and three mornings running he bought a newspaper and read the advertisements, to see whether there was any comfortable berth for a strong, good-'arted man wot didn't like work.

He actually went arter one situation, and, if it hadn't ha' been for seventy-nine other men, he said he believed he'd ha' had a good chance of getting it. As it was, all 'e got was a black eye for shoving another man, and for a day or two he was so down-'arted that 'e was no company at all for the other two.

For three or four days 'e went out by 'imself, and then, all of a sudden, Ginger Dick and Peter began to notice a great change in him. He seemed to 'ave got quite cheerful and 'appy. He answered 'em back pleasant when they spoke to 'im, and one night he lay in 'is bed whistling comic songs until Ginger and Peter Russet 'ad to get out o' bed to him. When he bought a new necktie and a smart cap and washed 'imself twice in one day they fust began to ask each other wot was up, and then they asked him.

"Up?" ses Sam; "nothing."

"He's in love," ses Peter Russet.

"You're a liar," ses Sam, without turning round.

"He'll 'ave it bad at 'is age," ses Ginger.

Sam didn't say nothing, but he kept fidgeting about as though 'e'd got something on his mind. Fust he looked out o' the winder, then he 'ummed a tune, and at last, looking at 'em very fierce, he took a tooth-brush wrapped in paper out of 'is pocket and began to clean 'is teeth.

"He is in love," ses Ginger, as soon as he could speak.

"Or else 'e's gorn mad," ses Peter, watching 'im. "Which is it, Sam?"

Sam made believe that he couldn't answer 'im because o' the tooth-brush, and arter he'd finished he 'ad such a raging toothache that 'e sat in a corner holding 'is face and looking the pictur' o' misery. They couldn't get a word out of him till they asked 'im to go out with them, and then he said 'e was going to bed. Twenty minutes arterwards, when Ginger Dick stepped back for 'is pipe, he found he 'ad gorn.

He tried the same game next night, but the other two wouldn't 'ave it, and they stayed in so long that at last 'e lost 'is temper, and, arter wondering wot Ginger's father and mother could ha' been a-thinking about, and saying that he believed Peter Russet 'ad been changed at birth for a sea-sick monkey, he put on 'is cap and went out. Both of 'em follered 'im sharp, but when he led 'em to a mission-hall, and actually went inside, they left 'im and went off on their own.

They talked it over that night between themselves, and next evening they went out fust and hid themselves round the corner. Ten minutes arterwards old Sam came out, walking as though 'e was going to catch a train; and smiling to think 'ow he 'ad shaken them off. At the corner of Commercial Road he stopped and bought 'imself a button-hole for 'is coat, and Ginger was so surprised that 'e pinched Peter Russet to make sure that he wasn't dreaming.

Old Sam walked straight on whistling, and every now and then looking down at 'is button-hole, until by-and-by he turned down a street on the right and went into a little shop. Ginger Dick and Peter waited for 'im at the corner, but he was inside for so long that at last they got tired o' waiting and crept up and peeped through the winder.

It was a little tobacconist's shop, with newspapers and penny toys and such-like; but, as far as Ginger could see through two rows o' pipes and the Police News, it was empty. They stood there with their noses pressed against the glass for some time, wondering wot had 'appened to Sam, but by-and-by a little boy went in and then they began to 'ave an idea wot Sam's little game was.

As the shop-bell went the door of a little parlour at the back of the shop opened, and a stout and uncommon good-looking woman of about forty came out. Her 'ead pushed the *Police News* out o' the way and her 'and came groping into the winder arter a toy.

Ginger 'ad a good look at 'er out o' the corner of one eye, while he pretended to be looking at a tobacco-jar with the other. As the little boy came out 'im and Peter Russet went in.

"I want a pipe, please," he ses, smiling at 'er; "a clay pipe—one o' your best." The woman handed 'im down a box to choose from, and just then Peter, wot 'ad been staring in at the arf-open door at a boot wot wanted lacing up, gave a big start and ses, "Why! Halloa!"

"Wot's the matter?" ses the woman, looking at 'im.

"I'd know that foot anywhere," ses Peter, still staring at it; and the words was hardly out of 'is mouth afore the foot 'ad moved itself away and tucked itself under its chair. "Why, that's my dear old friend Sam Small, ain't it?"

"Do you know the captin?" ses the woman, smiling at 'im.

"Cap—?" ses Peter. "Cap—? Oh, yes; why, he's the biggest friend I've got." "'Ow strange!" ses the woman.

"We've been wanting to see 'im for some time," ses Ginger. "He was kind enough to lend me arf a crown the other day, and I've been wanting to pay 'im."

"Captin Small," ses the woman, pushing open the door, "here's some old friends o' yours."

Old Sam turned 'is face round and looked at 'em, and if looks could ha' killed, as the saying is, they'd ha' been dead men there and then.

"Oh, yes," he ses, in a choking voice; "'ow are you?"

"Pretty well, thank you, captin," ses Ginger, grinning at 'im; "and 'ow's yourself arter all this long time?"

He held out 'is hand and Sam shook it, and then shook 'ands with Peter Russet, who was grinning so 'ard that he couldn't speak.

"These are two old friends o' mine, Mrs. Finch," ses old Sam, giving 'em a warning look; "Captin Dick and Captin Russet, two o' the oldest and best friends a man ever 'ad."

"Captin Dick 'as got arf a crown for you," ses Peter Russet, still grinning.

"There now," ses Ginger, looking vexed, "if I ain't been and forgot it; I've on'y got arf a sovereign."

"I can give you change, sir," ses Mrs. Finch. "P'r'aps you'd like to sit down for five minutes?"

Ginger thanked 'er, and 'im and Peter Russet took a chair apiece in front o' the fire and began asking old Sam about 'is 'ealth, and wot he'd been doing since they saw 'im last.

"Fancy your reckernizing his foot," ses Mrs. Finch, coming in with the change.

"I'd know it anywhere," ses Peter, who was watching Ginger pretending to give Sam Small the 'arf-dollar, and Sam pretending in a most lifelike manner to take it.

Ginger Dick looked round the room. It was a comfortable little place, with pictures on the walls and antimacassars on all the chairs, and a row of pink vases on the mantelpiece. Then 'e looked at Mrs. Finch, and thought wot a nice-looking woman she was.

"This is nicer than being aboard ship with a crew o' nasty, troublesome sailormen to look arter, Captin Small," he ses.

"It's wonderful the way he manages 'em," ses Peter Russet to Mrs. Finch. "Like a lion he is."

"A roaring lion," ses Ginger, looking at Sam. "He don't know wot fear is."

Sam began to smile, and Mrs. Finch looked at 'im so pleased that Peter Russet, who 'ad been looking at 'er and the room, and thinking much the same way as Ginger, began to think that they was on the wrong tack.

"Afore 'e got stout and old," he ses, shaking his 'ead, "there wasn't a smarter skipper afloat."

"We all 'ave our day," ses Ginger, shaking his 'ead too.

"I dessay he's good for another year or two afloat, yet," ses Peter Russet, considering. "With care," ses Ginger.

Old Sam was going to say something, but 'e stopped himself just in time. "They will 'ave their joke," he ses, turning to Mrs. Finch and trying to smile. "I feel as young as ever I did."

Mrs. Finch said that anybody with arf an eye could see that, and then she looked at a kettle that was singing on the 'ob.

"I s'pose you gentlemen wouldn't care for a cup o' cocoa?" she ses, turning to them.

Ginger Dick and Peter both said that they liked it better than anything else, and, arter she 'ad got out the cups and saucers and a tin o' cocoa, Ginger held the kettle and poured the water in the cups while she stirred them, and old Sam sat looking on 'elpless.

"It does seem funny to see you drinking cocoa, captin," ses Ginger, as old Sam took his cup.

"Ho!" ses Sam, firing up; "and why, if I might make so bold as to ask?"

"'Cos I've generally seen you drinking something out of a bottle," ses Ginger.

"Now, look 'ere," ses Sam, starting up and spilling some of the hot cocoa over 'is lap.

"A ginger-beer bottle," ses Peter Russet, making faces at Ginger to keep quiet.

"Yes, o' course, that's wot I meant," ses Ginger.

Old Sam wiped the cocoa off 'is knees without saying a word, but his weskit kept going up and down till Peter Russet felt quite sorry for 'im.

"There's nothing like it," he ses to Mrs. Finch. "It was by sticking to ginger-beer and milk and such-like that Captain Small 'ad command of a ship afore 'e was twenty-five."

"Lor'!" ses Mrs. Finch.

She smiled at old Sam till Peter got uneasy agin, and began to think p'r'aps 'e'd been praising 'im too much.

"Of course, I'm speaking of long ago now," he ses.

"Years and years afore you was born, ma'am," ses Ginger.

Old Sam was going to say something, but Mrs. Finch looked so pleased that 'e thought better of it. Some o' the cocoa 'e was drinking went the wrong way, and then Ginger patted 'im on the back and told 'im to be careful not to bring on 'is brownchitis agin. Wot with temper and being afraid to speak for fear they should let Mrs. Finch know that 'e wasn't a captin, he could 'ardly bear 'imself, but he very near broke out when Peter Russet advised 'im to 'ave his weskit lined with red flannel. They all stayed on till closing time, and by the time they left they 'ad made theirselves so pleasant that Mrs. Finch said she'd be pleased to see them any time they liked to look in.

Sam Small waited till they 'ad turned the corner, and then he broke out so alarming that they could 'ardly do anything with 'im. Twice policemen spoke to 'im and advised 'im to go home afore they altered their minds; and he 'ad to hold 'imself in and keep quiet while Ginger and Peter Russet took 'is arms and said they were seeing him 'ome.

He started the row agin when they got in-doors, and sat up in 'is bed smacking 'is lips over the things he'd like to 'ave done to them if he could. And then, arter saying 'ow he'd like to see Ginger boiled alive like a lobster, he said he knew that 'e was a noble-'arted feller who wouldn't try and cut an old pal out, and that it was a case of love at first sight on top of a tram-car.

"She's too young for you," ses Ginger; "and too good-looking besides."

"It's the nice little bisness he's fallen in love with, Ginger," ses Peter Russet. "I'll toss you who 'as it."

Ginger, who was siting on the foot o' Sam's bed, said "no" at fust, but arter a time he pulled out arf a dollar and spun it in the air.

That was the last 'e see of it, although he 'ad Sam out o' bed and all the clothes stripped off of it twice. He spent over arf an hour on his 'ands and knees looking for it, and Sam said when he was tired of playing bears p'r'aps he'd go to bed and get to sleep like a Christian.

They 'ad it all over agin next morning, and at last, as nobody would agree to keep quiet and let the others 'ave a fair chance, they made up their minds to let the best man win. Ginger Dick bought a necktie that took all the colour out o' Sam's, and Peter Russet went in for a collar so big that 'e was lost in it.

They all strolled into the widow's shop separate that night. Ginger Dick 'ad smashed his pipe and wanted another; Peter Russet wanted some tobacco; and old Sam Small walked in smiling, with a little silver brooch for 'er, that he said 'e had picked up.

It was a very nice brooch, and Mrs. Finch was so pleased with it that Ginger and Peter sat there as mad as they could be because they 'adn't thought of the same thing.

"Captain Small is very lucky at finding things," ses Ginger, at last.

"He's got the name for it," ses Peter Russet.

"It's a handy 'abit," ses Ginger; "it saves spending money. Who did you give that gold bracelet to you picked up the other night, captin?" he ses, turning to Sam.

"Gold bracelet?" ses Sam. "I didn't pick up no gold bracelet. Wot are you talking about?"

"All right, captin; no offence," ses Ginger, holding up his 'and. "I dreamt I saw one on your mantelpiece, I s'pose. P'r'aps I oughtn't to ha' said anything about it."

Old Sam looked as though he'd like to eat 'im, especially as he noticed Mrs. Finch listening and pretending not to. "Oh! that one," he ses, arter a bit o' hard thinking. "Oh! I found out who it belonged to. You wouldn't believe 'ow pleased they was at getting it back agin."

Ginger Dick coughed and began to think as 'ow old Sam was sharper than he 'ad given 'im credit for, but afore he could think of anything else to say Mrs. Finch looked at old Sam and began to talk about 'is ship, and to say 'ow much she should like to see over it.

"I wish I could take you," ses Sam, looking at the other two out o' the corner of his eye, "but my ship's over at Dunkirk, in France. I've just run over to London for a week or two to look round."

"And mine's there too," ses Peter Russet, speaking a'most afore old Sam 'ad finished; "side by side they lay in the harbour."

"Oh, dear," ses Mrs. Finch, folding her 'ands and shaking her 'ead. "I should like to go over a ship one arternoon. I'd quite made up my mind to it, knowing three captins."

She smiled and looked at Ginger; and Sam and Peter looked at 'im too, wondering whether he was going to berth his ship at Dunkirk alongside o' theirs.

"Ah, I wish I 'ad met you a fortnight ago," ses Ginger, very sad. "I gave up my ship, the High flyer, then, and I'm waiting for one my owners are 'aving built for me at New-castle. They said the High flyer wasn't big enough for me. She was a nice little ship, though. I believe I've got 'er picture somewhere about me!"

He felt in 'is pocket and pulled out a little, crumpled-up photograph of a ship he'd been fireman aboard of some years afore, and showed it to 'er.

"That's me standing on the bridge," he ses, pointing out a little dot with the stem of 'is pipe.

"It's your figger," ses Mrs. Finch, straining her eyes. "I should know it anywhere."

"You've got wonderful eyes, ma'am," ses old Sam, choking with 'is pipe.

"Anybody can see that," ses Ginger. "They're the largest and the bluest I've ever seen."

Mrs. Finch told 'im not to talk nonsense, but both Sam and Peter Russet could see 'ow pleased she was.

"Truth is truth," ses Ginger. "I'm a plain man, and I speak my mind."

"Blue is my fav'rit' colour," ses old Sam, in a tender voice. "True blue."

Peter Russet began to feel out of it. "I thought brown was," he ses.

"Ho!" ses Sam, turning on 'im; "and why?"

"I 'ad my reasons," ses Peter, nodding, and shutting 'is mouth very firm.

"I thought brown was 'is fav'rit colour too," ses Ginger. "I don't know why. It's no use asking me; because if you did I couldn't tell you."

"Brown's a very nice colour," ses Mrs. Finch, wondering wot was the matter with old Sam.

"Blue," ses Ginger; "big blue eyes—they're the ones for me. Other people may 'ave their blacks and their browns," he ses, looking at Sam and Peter Russet, "but give me blue."

They went on like that all the evening, and every time the shop-bell went and the widow 'ad to go out to serve a customer they said in w'ispers wot they thought of each other; and once when she came back rather sudden Ginger 'ad to explain to 'er that 'e was showing Peter Russet a scratch on his knuckle.

Ginger Dick was the fust there next night, and took 'er a little chiney teapot he 'ad picked up dirt cheap because it was cracked right across the middle; but, as he explained that he 'ad dropped it in hurrying to see 'er, she was just as pleased. She stuck it up on the mantelpiece, and the things she said about Ginger's kindness and generosity made Peter Russet spend good money that he wanted for 'imself on a painted flower-pot next evening.

With three men all courting 'er at the same time Mrs. Finch had 'er hands full, but she took to it wonderful considering. She was so nice and kind to 'em all that even arter a week's 'ard work none of 'em was really certain which she liked best.

They took to going in at odd times o' the day for tobacco and such-like. They used to go alone then, but they all met and did the polite to each other there of an evening, and then quarrelled all the way 'ome.

Then all of a sudden, without any warning, Ginger Dick and Peter Russet left off going there. The fust evening Sam sat expecting them every minute, and was so surprised that he couldn't take any advantage of it; but on the second, beginning by squeezing Mrs. Finch's 'and at ha'-past seven, he 'ad got best part of his arm round 'er waist by a quarter to ten. He didn't do more that night because she told him to be'ave 'imself, and threatened to scream if he didn't leave off.

He was arf-way home afore 'e thought of the reason for Ginger Dick and Peter Russet giving up, and then he went along smiling to 'imself to such an extent that people thought 'e was mad. He went off to sleep with the smile still on 'is lips, and when Peter and Ginger came in soon arter closing time and 'e woke up and asked them where they'd been, 'e was still smiling.

"I didn't 'ave the pleasure o' seeing you at Mrs. Finch's to-night," he ses.

"No," ses Ginger, very short. "We got tired of it."

"So un'ealthy sitting in that stuffy little room every evening," ses Peter.

Old Sam put his 'ead under the bedclothes and laughed till the bed shook; and every now and then he'd put his 'ead out and look at Peter and Ginger and laugh agin till he choked.

"I see 'ow it is," he ses, sitting up and wiping his eyes on the sheet. "Well, we cant all win."

"Wot d'ye mean?" ses Ginger, very disagreeable.

"She wouldn't 'ave you, Sam, thats wot I mean. And I don't wonder at it. I wouldn't 'ave you if I was a gal."

"You're dreaming, ses Peter Russet, sneering at 'im.

"That flower-pot o' yours'll come in handy," ses Sam, thinking 'ow he 'ad put 'is arm round the widow's waist; "and I thank you kindly for the teapot, Ginger.

"You don't mean to say as you've asked 'er to marry you?" ses Ginger, looking at Peter Russet.

"Not quite; but I'm going to," ses Sam, "and I'll bet you even arf-crowns she ses 'yes.'"

Ginger wouldn't take 'im, and no more would Peter, not even when he raised it to five shillings; and the vain way old Sam lay there boasting and talking about 'is way with the gals made 'em both feel ill.

"I wouldn't 'ave her if she asked me on 'er bended knees," ses Ginger, holding up his 'ead.

"Nor me," ses Peter. "You're welcome to 'er, Sam. When I think of the evenings I've wasted over a fat old woman I feel—"

"That'll do," ses old Sam, very sharp; "that ain't the way to speak of a lady, even if she 'as said 'no.'"

"All right, Sam," ses Ginger. "You go in and win if you think you're so precious clever."

Old Sam said that that was wot 'e was going to do, and he spent so much time next morning making 'imself look pretty that the other two could 'ardly be civil to him.

He went off a'most direckly arter breakfast, and they didn't see 'im agin till twelve o'clock that night. He 'ad brought a bottle o' whisky in with 'im, and he was so 'appy that they see plain wot had 'appened.

"She said 'yes' at two o'clock in the arternoon," ses old Sam, smiling, arter they had 'ad a glass apiece. "I'd nearly done the trick at one o'clock, and then the shop-bell went, and I 'ad to begin all over agin. Still, it wasn't unpleasant."

"Do you mean to tell us you've asked 'er to marry you?" ses Ginger, 'olding out 'is glass to be filled agin.

"I do," ses Sam; "but I 'ope there's no ill-feeling. You never 'ad a chance, neither of you; she told me so."

Ginger Dick and Peter Russet stared at each other.

"She said she 'ad been in love with me all along," ses Sam, filling their glasses agin to cheer 'em up. "We went out arter tea and bought the engagement-ring, and then she got somebody to mind the shop and we went to the Pagoda music-'all."

"I 'ope you didn't pay much for the ring, Sam," ses Ginger, who always got very kind-'arted arter two or three glasses o' whisky. "If I'd known you was going to be in such a hurry I might ha' told you before."

"We ought to ha' done," ses Peter, shaking his 'ead.

"Told me?" ses Sam, staring at 'em. "Told me wot?"

"Why me and Peter gave it up," ses Ginger; "but, o' course, p'r'aps you don't mind."

"Mind wot?" ses Sam.

"It's wonderful 'ow quiet she kept it," ses Peter.

Old Sam stared at 'em agin, and then he asked 'em to speak in plain English wot they'd got to say, and not to go taking away the character of a woman wot wasn't there to speak up for herself.

"It's nothing agin 'er character," ses Ginger. "It's a credit to her, looked at properly," ses Peter Russet.

"And Sam'll 'ave the pleasure of bringing of 'em up," ses Ginger.

"Bringing of 'em up?" ses Sam, in a trembling voice and turning pale; "bringing who up?"

"Why, 'er children," ses Ginger. "Didn't she tell you? She's got nine of 'em."

Sam pretended not to believe 'em at fust, and said they was jealous; but next day he crept down to the greengrocer's shop in the same street, where Ginger had 'appened to buy some oranges one day, and found that it was only too true. Nine children, the eldest of 'em only fifteen, was staying with diff'rent relations owing to scarlet-fever next door.

Old Sam crept back 'ome like a man in a dream, with a bag of oranges he didn't want, and, arter making a present of the engagement-ring to Ginger—if 'e could get it—he took the fust train to Tilbury and signed on for a v'y'ge to China.

THE CASTAWAY

Mrs. John Boxer stood at the door of the shop with her hands clasped on her apron. The short day had drawn to a close, and the lamps in the narrow little thorough-fares of Shinglesea were already lit. For a time she stood listening to the regular beat of the sea on the beach some half-mile distant, and then with a slight shiver stepped back into the shop and closed the door.

The little shop with its wide-mouthed bottles of sweets was one of her earliest memories. Until her marriage she had known no other home, and when her husband was lost with the *North Star* some three years before, she gave up her home in Poplar and returned to assist her mother in the little shop.

In a restless mood she took up a piece of needle-work, and a minute or two later put it down again. A glance through the glass of the door leading into the small parlour revealed Mrs. Gimpson, with a red shawl round her shoulders, asleep in her easy-chair.

Mrs. Boxer turned at the clang of the shop bell, and then, with a wild cry, stood gazing at the figure of a man standing in the door-way. He was short and bearded, with oddly shaped shoulders, and a left leg which was not a match; but the next moment Mrs. Boxer was in his arms sobbing and laughing together.

Mrs. Gimpson, whose nerves were still quivering owing to the suddenness with which she had been awakened, came into the shop; Mr. Boxer freed an arm, and placing it round her waist kissed her with some affection on the chin.

"He's come back!" cried Mrs. Boxer, hysterically.

"Thank goodness," said Mrs. Gimpson, after a moment's deliberation.

"He's alive!" cried Mrs. Boxer. "He's alive !"

She half-dragged and half-led him into the small parlour, and thrusting him into the easy-chair lately vacated by Mrs. Gimpson seated herself upon his knee, regardless in her excitement that the rightful owner was with elaborate care selecting the most uncomfortable chair in the room.

"Fancy his coming back!" said Mrs. Boxer, wiping her eyes. "How did you escape, John? Where have you been? Tell us all about it."

Mr. Boxer sighed. "It 'ud be a long story if I had the gift of telling of it," he said, slowly, "but I'll cut it short for the present. When the *North Star* went down in the South Pacific most o' the hands got away in the boats, but I was too late. I got this crack on the head with something falling on it from aloft. Look here."

He bent his head, and Mrs. Boxer, separating the stubble with her fingers, uttered an exclamation of pity and alarm at the extent of the scar; Mrs. Gimpson, craning forward, uttered a sound which might mean anything—even pity.

"When I come to my senses," continued Mr. Boxer, "the ship was sinking, and I just got to my feet when she went down and took me with her. How I escaped I don't know. I seemed to be choking and fighting for my breath for years, and then I found myself floating on the sea and clinging to a grating. I clung to it all night, and next day I was picked up by a native who was paddling about in a canoe, and taken ashore to an island, where I lived for over two years. It was right out o' the way o' craft, but at last I was picked up by a trading schooner named the *Pearl,* belonging to Sydney, and taken there. At Sydney I shipped aboard the *Marston Towers,* a steamer, and landed at the Albert Docks this morning."

"Poor John," said his wife, holding on to his arm. "How you must have suffered!"

"I did," said Mr. Boxer. "Mother got a cold?" he inquired, eying that lady.

"No, I ain't," said Mrs. Gimpson, answering for herself. "Why didn't you write when you got to Sydney?"

"Didn't know where to write to," replied Mr. Boxer, staring. "I didn't know where Mary had gone to."

"You might ha' wrote here," said Mrs. Gimpson.

"Didn't think of it at the time," said Mr. Boxer. "One thing is, I was very busy at Sydney, looking for a ship. However, I'm 'ere now."

"I always felt you'd turn up some day," said Mrs. Gimpson. "I felt certain of it in my own mind. Mary made sure you was dead, but I said 'no, I knew better.'"

There was something in Mrs. Gimpson's manner of saying this that impressed her listeners unfavourably. The impression was deepened when, after a short, dry laugh *a propos* of nothing, she sniffed again—three times.

"Well, you turned out to be right," said Mr. Boxer, shortly.

"I gin'rally am," was the reply; "there's very few people can take me in."

She sniffed again.

"Were the natives kind to you?" inquired Mrs. Boxer, hastily, as she turned to her husband.

"Very kind," said the latter. "Ah! you ought to have seen that island. Beautiful yellow sands and palm-trees; cocoa-nuts to be 'ad for the picking, and nothing to do all day but lay about in the sun and swim in the sea."

"Any public-'ouses there?" inquired Mrs. Gimpson.

"Cert'nly not," said her son-in-law. "This was an island—one o' the little islands in the South Pacific Ocean."

"What did you say the name o' the schooner was?" inquired Mrs. Gimpson.

"*Pearl,*" replied Mr. Boxer, with the air of a resentful witness under cross-examination.

"And what was the name o' the captin?" said Mrs. Gimpson.

"Thomas—Henery—Walter—Smith," said Mr. Boxer, with somewhat unpleasant emphasis.

"An' the mate's name?"

"John Brown," was the reply.

"Common names," commented Mrs. Gimpson, "very common. But I knew you'd come back all right—I never 'ad no alarm. 'He's safe and happy, my dear,' I says. 'He'll come back all in his own good time.'"

"What d'you mean by that?" demanded the sensitive Mr. Boxer. "I come back as soon as I could."

"You know you were anxious, mother," interposed her daughter. "Why, you insisted upon our going to see old Mr. Silver about it."

"Ah! but I wasn't uneasy or anxious afterwards," said Mrs. Gimpson, compressing her lips.

"Who's old Mr. Silver, and what should he know about it?" inquired Mr. Boxer.

"He's a fortune-teller," replied his wife. "Reads the stars," said his mother-in-law.

Mr. Boxer laughed—a good ringing laugh. "What did he tell you?" he inquired. "Nothing," said his wife, hastily. "Ah!" said Mr. Boxer, waggishly, "that was wise of 'im. Most of us could tell fortunes that way."

"That's wrong," said Mrs. Gimpson to her daughter, sharply. "Right's right any day, and truth's truth. He said that he knew all about John and what he'd been doing, but he wouldn't tell us for fear of 'urting our feelings and making mischief."

"Here, look 'ere," said Mr. Boxer, starting up; "I've 'ad about enough o' this. Why don't you speak out what you mean? I'll mischief 'im, the old humbug. Old rascal."

"Never mind, John," said his wife, laying her hand upon his arm. "Here you are safe and sound, and as for old Mr. Silver, there's a lot o' people don't believe in him."

"Ah! they don't want to," said Mrs. Gimpson, obstinately. "But don't forget that he foretold my cough last winter."

"Well, look 'ere," said Mr. Boxer, twisting his short, blunt nose into as near an imitation of a sneer as he could manage, "I've told you my story and I've got witnesses to prove it. You can write to the master of the Marston Towers if you like, and other people besides. Very well, then; let's go and see your precious old fortune-teller. You needn't say who I am; say I'm a friend, and tell 'im never to mind about making mischief, but to say right out where I am and what I've been doing all this time. I have my 'opes it'll cure you of your superstitiousness."

"We'll go round after we've shut up, mother," said Mrs. Boxer. "We'll have a bit o' supper first and then start early."

Mrs. Gimpson hesitated. It is never pleasant to submit one's superstitions to the tests of the unbelieving, but after the attitude she had taken up she was extremely loath to allow her son-in-law a triumph.

"Never mind, we'll say no more about it," she said, primly, "but I 'ave my own ideas."

"I dessay," said Mr. Boxer; "but you're afraid for us to go to your old fortune-teller. It would be too much of a show-up for 'im."

"It's no good your trying to aggravate me, John Boxer, because you can't do it," said Mrs. Gimpson, in a voice trembling with passion.

"O' course, if people like being deceived they must be," said Mr. Boxer; "we've all got to live, and if we'd all got our common sense fortune-tellers couldn't. Does he tell fortunes by tea-leaves or by the colour of your eyes?"

"Laugh away, John Boxer," said Mrs. Gimpson, icily; "but I shouldn't have been alive now if it hadn't ha' been for Mr. Silver's warnings."

"Mother stayed in bed for the first ten days in July," explained Mrs. Boxer, "to avoid being bit by a mad dog."

"Tchee—tchee—tchee," said the hapless Mr. Boxer, putting his hand over his mouth and making noble efforts to restrain himself; "tchee—tch

"I s'pose you'd ha' laughed more if I 'ad been bit?" said the glaring Mrs. Gimpson.

"Well, who did the dog bite after all?" inquired Mr. Boxer, recovering.

"You don't understand," replied Mrs. Gimpson, pityingly; "me being safe up in bed and the door locked, there was no mad dog. There was no use for it."

"Well," said Mr. Boxer, "me and Mary's going round to see that old deceiver after supper, whether you come or not. Mary shall tell 'im I'm a friend, and ask him to tell her everything about 'er husband. Nobody knows me here, and Mary and me'll be affectionate like, and give 'im to understand we want to marry. Then he won't mind making mischief."

"You'd better leave well alone," said Mrs. Gimpson.

Mr. Boxer shook his head. "I was always one for a bit o' fun," he said, slowly. "I want to see his face when he finds out who I am."

Mrs. Gimpson made no reply; she was looking round for the market-basket, and having found it she left the reunited couple to keep house while she went out to obtain a supper which should, in her daughter's eyes, be worthy of the occasion.

She went to the High Street first and made her purchases, and was on the way back again when, in response to a sudden impulse, as she passed the end of Crowner's Alley, she turned into that small by-way and knocked at the astrologer's door.

A slow, dragging footstep was heard approaching in reply to the summons, and the astrologer, recognising his visitor as one of his most faithful and credulous clients, invited her to step inside. Mrs. Gimpson complied, and, taking a chair, gazed at the venerable white beard and small, red-rimmed eyes of her host in some perplexity as to how to begin.

"My daughter's coming round to see you presently," she said, at last.

The astrologer nodded.

"She—she wants to ask you about 'er husband," faltered' Mrs. Gimpson; "she's going to bring a friend with her—a man who doesn't believe in your knowledge. He—he knows all about my daughter's husband, and he wants to see what you say you know about him."

The old man put on a pair of huge horn spectacles and eyed her carefully.

"You've got something on your mind," he said, at last; "you'd better tell me everything."

Mrs. Gimpson shook her head.

"There's some danger hanging over you," continued Mr. Silver, in a low, thrilling voice; "some danger in connection with your son-in-law. There" he waved a lean, shrivelled hand backward and for-ward as though dispelling a fog, and peered into distance—"there is something forming over you. You—or somebody—are hiding something from me."

Mrs. Gimpson, aghast at such omniscience, sank backward in her chair.

"Speak," said the old man, gently; "there is no reason why you should be sacrificed for others."

Mrs. Gimpson was of the same opinion, and in some haste she reeled off the events of the evening. She had a good memory, and no detail was lost.

"Strange, strange," said the venerable Mr. Silver, when he had finished. "He is an ingenious man."

"Isn't it true?" inquired his listener. "He says he can prove it. And he is going to find out what you meant by saying you were afraid of making mischief."

"He can prove some of it," said the old man, his eyes snapping spitefully. "I can guarantee that."

"But it wouldn't have made mischief if you had told us that," ventured Mrs. Gimpson. "A man can't help being cast away."

"True," said the astrologer, slowly; "true. But let them come and question me; and whatever you do, for your own sake don't let a soul know that you have been here. If you do, the danger to yourself will be so terrible that even I may be unable to help you."

Mrs. Gimpson shivered, and more than ever impressed by his marvellous powers made her way slowly home, where she found the unconscious Mr. Boxer relating his adventures again with much gusto to a married couple from next door.

"It's a wonder he's alive," said Mr. Jem Thompson, looking up as the old woman entered the room; "it sounds like a story-book. Show us that cut on your head again, mate."

The obliging Mr. Boxer complied.

"We're going on with 'em after they've 'ad sup-per," continued Mr. Thompson, as he and his wife rose to depart. "It'll be a fair treat to me to see old Silver bowled out."

Mrs. Gimpson sniffed and eyed his retreating figure disparagingly; Mrs. Boxer, prompted by her husband, began to set the table for supper.

It was a lengthy meal, owing principally to Mr. Boxer, but it was over at last, and after that gentleman had assisted in shutting up the shop they joined the Thompsons, who were waiting outside, and set off for Crowner's Alley. The way was enlivened by Mr. Boxer, who had thrills of horror every ten yards at the idea of the supernatural things he was about to witness, and by Mr. Thompson, who, not to be outdone, persisted in standing stock-still at frequent intervals until he had received the assurances of his giggling better-half that he would not be made to vanish in a cloud of smoke.

By the time they reached Mr. Silver's abode the party had regained its decorum, and, except for a tremendous shudder on the part of Mr. Boxer as his gaze fell on a couple of skulls which decorated the magician's table, their behaviour left nothing to be desired. Mrs. Gimpson, in a few awkward words, announced the occasion of their visit. Mr. Boxer she introduced as a friend of the family from London.

"I will do what I can," said the old man, slowly, as his visitors seated themselves, "but I can only tell you what I see. If I do not see all, or see clearly, it cannot be helped."

Mr. Boxer winked at Mr. Thompson, and received an understanding pinch in return; Mrs. Thompson in a hot whisper told them to behave themselves.

The mystic preparations were soon complete. A little cloud of smoke, through which the fierce red eyes of the astrologer peered keenly at Mr. Boxer, rose from the table. Then he poured various liquids into a small china bowl and, holding up his hand to command silence, gazed steadfastly into it. "I see pictures," he announced, in a deep voice. "The docks of a great city; London. I see an ill-shaped man with a bent left leg standing on the deck of a ship."

Mr. Thompson, his eyes wide open with surprise, jerked Mr. Boxer in the ribs, but Mr. Boxer, whose figure was a sore point with him, made no response.

"The ship leaves the docks," continued Mr. Silver, still peering into the bowl. "As she passes through the entrance her stern comes into view with the name painted on it. The—the—the—"

"Look agin, old chap," growled Mr. Boxer, in an undertone.

"The North Star," said the astrologer. "The ill-shaped man is still standing on the fore-part of the ship; I do not know his name or who he is. He takes the portrait of a beautiful young woman from his pocket and gazes at it earnestly."

Mrs. Boxer, who had no illusions on the subject of her personal appearance, sat up as though she had been stung; Mr. Thompson, who was about to nudge Mr. Boxer in the ribs again, thought better of it and assumed an air of uncompromising virtue.

"The picture disappears," said Mr. Silver. "Ah! I see; I see. A ship in a gale at sea. It is the North Star; it is sinking. The ill-shaped man sheds tears and loses his head. I cannot discover the name of this man."

Mr. Boxer, who had been several times on the point of interrupting, cleared his throat and endeavoured to look unconcerned.

"The ship sinks," continued the astrologer, in thrilling tones. "Ah! what is this? a piece of wreck-age with a monkey clinging to it? No, no-o. The ill-shaped man again. Dear me!"

His listeners sat spellbound. Only the laboured and intense breathing of Mr. Boxer broke the silence.

"He is alone on the boundless sea," pursued the seer; "night falls. Day breaks, and a canoe propelled by a slender and pretty but dusky maiden approaches the castaway. She assists him into the canoe and his head sinks on her lap, as with vigorous strokes of her paddle she propels the canoe toward a small island fringed with palm trees."

"Here, look 'ere—" began the overwrought Mr. Boxer.

"H'sh, h'sh!" ejaculated the keenly interested Mr. Thompson. "W'y don't you keep quiet?"

"The picture fades," continued the old man. "I see another: a native wedding. It is the dusky maiden and the man she rescued. Ah! the wedding is interrupted; a young man, a native, breaks into the group. He has a long knife in his hand. He springs upon the ill-shaped man and wounds him in the head."

Involuntarily Mr. Boxer's hand went up to his honourable scar, and the heads of the others swung round to gaze at it. Mrs. Boxer's face was terrible in its expression, but Mrs. Gimpson's bore the look of sad and patient triumph of one who knew men and could not be surprised at anything they do.

"The scene vanishes," resumed the monotonous voice, "and another one forms. The same man stands on the deck of a small ship. The name on the stern is the Peer—no, Paris—no, no, no, Pearl. It fades from the shore where the dusky maiden stands with hands stretched out imploringly. The ill-shaped man smiles and takes the portrait of the young and beautiful girl from his pocket."

"Look 'ere," said the infuriated Mr. Boxer, "I think we've 'ad about enough of this rubbish. I have— more than enough."

"I don't wonder at it," said his wife, trembling furiously. "You can go if you like. I'm going to stay and hear all that there is to hear."

"You sit quiet," urged the intensely interested Mr. Thompson. "He ain't said it's you. There's more than one misshaped man in the world, I s'pose?"

"I see an ocean liner," said the seer, who had appeared to be in a trance state during this colloquy. "She is sailing for England from Australia. I see the name distinctly: the *Marston Towers*. The same man is on board of her. The ship arrives at London. The scene closes; another one forms. The ill-shaped man is sitting with a woman with a beautiful face —not the same as the photograph."

"What they can see in him I can't think," muttered Mr. Thompson, in an envious whisper. "He's a perfick terror, and to look at him—"

"They sit hand in hand," continued the astrologer, raising his voice. "She smiles up at him and gently strokes his head; he—"

A loud smack rang through the room and startled the entire company; Mrs. Boxer, unable to contain herself any longer, had, so far from profiting by the example, gone to the other extreme and slapped her husband's head with hearty good-will. Mr. Boxer sprang raging to his feet, and in the confusion which ensued the fortune-teller, to the great regret of Mr. Thompson, upset the contents of the magic bowl.

"I can see no more," he said, sinking hastily into his chair behind the table as Mr. Boxer advanced upon him.

Mrs. Gimpson pushed her son-in-law aside, and laying a modest fee upon the table took her daughter's arm and led her out. The Thompsons followed, and Mr. Boxer, after an irresolute glance in the direction of the ingenuous Mr. Silver, made his way after them and fell into the rear. The people in front walked on for some time in silence, and then the voice of the greatly impressed Mrs.

Thompson was heard, to the effect that if there were only more fortune-tellers in the world there would be a lot more better men.

Mr. Boxer trotted up to his wife's side. "Look here, Mary," he began.

"Don't you speak to me," said his wife, drawing closer to her mother, "because I won't answer you."

Mr. Boxer laughed, bitterly. "This is a nice home-coming," he remarked.

He fell to the rear again and walked along raging, his temper by no means being improved by observing that Mrs. Thompson, doubtless with a firm belief in the saying that "Evil communications corrupt good manners," kept a tight hold of her husband's arm. His position as an outcast was clearly defined, and he ground his teeth with rage as he observed the virtuous uprightness of Mrs. Gimpson's back. By the time they reached home he was in a spirit of mad recklessness far in advance of the character given him by the astrologer.

His wife gazed at him with a look of such strong interrogation as he was about to follow her into the house that he paused with his foot on the step and eyed her dumbly.

"Have you left anything inside that you want?" she inquired.

Mr. Boxer shook his head. "I only wanted to come in and make a clean breast of it," he said, in a curious voice; "then I'll go."

Mrs. Gimpson stood aside to let him pass, and Mr. Thompson, not to be denied, followed close behind with his faintly protesting wife. They sat down in a row against the wall, and Mr. Boxer, sitting opposite in a hang-dog fashion, eyed them with scornful wrath.

"Well?" said Mrs. Boxer, at last.

"All that he said was quite true," said her husband, defiantly. "The only thing is, he didn't tell the arf of it. Altogether, I married three dusky maidens."

Everybody but Mr. Thompson shuddered with horror.

"Then I married a white girl in Australia," pursued Mr. Boxer, musingly. "I wonder old Silver didn't see that in the bowl; not arf a fortune-teller, I call 'im."

"What they see in 'im!" whispered the astounded Mr. Thompson to his wife.

"And did you marry the beautiful girl in the photograph?" demanded Mrs. Boxer, in trembling accents.

"I did," said her husband.

"Hussy," cried Mrs. Boxer.

"I married her," said Mr. Boxer, considering—"I married her at Camberwell, in eighteen ninety-three."

"Eighteen ninety-three!" said his wife, in a startled voice. "But you couldn't. Why, you didn't marry me till eighteen ninety-four."

"What's that got to do with it?" inquired the monster, calmly.

Mrs. Boxer, pale as ashes, rose from her seat and stood gazing at him with horror-struck eyes, trying in vain to speak.

"You villain!" cried Mrs. Gimpson, violently. "I always distrusted you."

"I know you did," said Mr. Boxer, calmly. "You've been committing bigamy," cried Mrs. Gimpson.

"Over and over agin," assented Mr. Boxer, cheerfully. "It's got to be a 'obby with me."

"Was the first wife alive when you married my daughter?" demanded Mrs. Gimpson.

"Alive?" said Mr. Boxer. "O' course she was. She's alive now—bless her."

He leaned back in his chair and regarded with intense satisfaction the horrified faces of the group in front.

"You—you'll go to jail for this," cried Mrs. Gimpson, breathlessly. "What is your first wife's address?"

"I decline to answer that question," said her son-in-law.

"What is your first wife's address?" repeated Mrs. Gimpson.

"Ask the fortune-teller," said Mr. Boxer, with an aggravating smile. "And then get 'im up in the box as a witness, little bowl and all. He can tell you more than I can."

"I demand to know her name and address," cried Mrs. Gimpson, putting a bony arm around the waist of the trembling Mrs. Boxer.

"I decline to give it," said Mr. Boxer, with great relish. "It ain't likely I'm going to give myself away like that; besides, it's agin the law for a man to criminate himself. You go on and start your bigamy case, and call old red-eyes as a witness."

Mrs. Gimpson gazed at him in speechless wrath and then stooping down conversed in excited whispers with Mrs. Thompson. Mrs. Boxer crossed over to her husband.

"Oh, John," she wailed, "say it isn't true, say it isn't true."

Mr. Boxer hesitated. "What's the good o' me saying anything?" he said, doggedly.

"It isn't true," persisted his wife. "Say it isn't true."

"What I told you when I first came in this evening was quite true," said her husband, slowly. "And what I've just told you is as true as what that lying old fortune-teller told you. You can please yourself what you believe."

"I believe you, John," said his wife, humbly.

Mr. Boxer's countenance cleared and he drew her on to his knee.

"That's right," he said, cheerfully. "So long as you believe in me I don't care what other people think. And before I'm much older I'll find out how that old rascal got to know the names of the ships I was aboard. Seems to me somebody's been talking."

THE CHANGELING

Mr. George Henshaw let himself in at the front door, and stood for some time wiping his boots on the mat. The little house was ominously still, and a faint feeling, only partially due to the lapse of time since breakfast, manifested itself behind his waistcoat. He coughed—a matter-of-fact cough— and, with an attempt to hum a tune, hung his hat on the peg and entered the kitchen.

Mrs. Henshaw had just finished dinner. The neatly cleaned bone of a chop was on a plate by her side; a small dish which had contained a rice-pudding was empty; and the only food left on the table was a small rind of cheese and a piece of stale bread. Mr. Henshaw's face fell, but he drew his chair up to the table and waited.

His wife regarded him with a fixed and offensive stare. Her face was red and her eyes were blazing. It was hard to ignore her gaze; harder still to meet it. Mr. Henshaw, steering a middle course, allowed his eyes to wander round the room and to dwell, for the fraction of a second, on her angry face.

"You've had dinner early?" he said at last, in a trembling voice.

"Have I?" was the reply.

Mr. Henshaw sought for a comforting explanation. "Clock's fast," he said, rising and adjusting it.

His wife rose almost at the same moment, and with slow deliberate movements began to clear the table.

"What—what about dinner?" said Mr. Henshaw, still trying to control his fears.

"Dinner!" repeated Mrs. Henshaw, in a terrible voice. "You go and tell that creature you were on the 'bus with to get your dinner."

Mr. Henshaw made a gesture of despair. "I tell you," he said emphatically, "it wasn't me. I told you so last night. You get an idea in your head and—"

"That'll do," said his wife, sharply. "I saw you, George Henshaw, as plain as I see you now. You were tickling her ear with a bit o' straw, and that good-for-nothing friend of yours, Ted Stokes, was sitting behind with another beauty. Nice way o' going on, and me at 'ome all alone by myself, slaving and slaving to keep things respectable!"

"It wasn't me," reiterated the unfortunate.

"When I called out to you," pursued the unheeding Mrs. Henshaw, "you started and pulled your hat over your eyes and turned away. I should have caught you if it hadn't been for all them carts in the way and falling down. I can't understand now how it was I wasn't killed; I was a mask of mud from head to foot."

Despite his utmost efforts to prevent it, a faint smile flitted across the pallid features of Mr. Henshaw.

"Yes, you may laugh," stormed his wife, "and I've no doubt them two beauties laughed too. I'll take care you don't have much more to laugh at, my man."

She flung out of the room and began to wash up the crockery. Mr. Henshaw, after standing irresolute for some time with his hands in his pockets, put on his hat again and left the house.

He dined badly at a small eating-house, and returned home at six o'clock that evening to find his wife out and the cupboard empty. He went back to the same restaurant for tea, and after a gloomy meal went round to discuss the situation with Ted Stokes. That gentleman's suggestion of a double alibi he thrust aside with disdain and a stern appeal to talk sense.

"Mind, if my wife speaks to you about it," he said, warningly, "it wasn't me, but somebody like me. You might say he 'ad been mistook for me before."

Mr. Stokes grinned and, meeting a freezing glance from his friend, at once became serious again.

"Why not say it was you?" he said stoutly. "There's no harm in going for a 'bus-ride with a friend and a couple o' ladies."

"O' course there ain't," said the other, hotly, "else I shouldn't ha' done it. But you know what my wife is. '

Mr. Stokes, who was by no means a favorite of the lady in question, nodded. "You were a bit larky, too," he said thoughtfully. "You 'ad quite a little slapping game after you pretended to steal her brooch."

"I s'pose when a gentleman's with a lady he 'as got to make 'imself pleasant?" said Mr. Henshaw, with dignity. "Now, if my missis speaks to you about it, you say that it wasn't me, but a friend of yours up from the country who is as like me as two peas. See?"

"Name o' Dodd," said Mr. Stokes, with a knowing nod. "Tommy Dodd."

"I'm not playing the giddy goat," said the other, bitterly, "and I'd thank you not to."

"All right," said Mr. Stokes, somewhat taken aback. "Any name you like; I don't mind."

Mr. Henshaw pondered. "Any sensible name'll do," he said, stiffly.

"Bell?" suggested Mr. Stokes. "Alfred Bell? I did know a man o' that name once. He tried to borrow a bob off of me."

"That'll do," said his friend, after some consideration; "but mind you stick to the same name. And you'd better make up something about him—where he lives, and all that sort of thing—so that you can stand being questioned without looking more like a silly fool than you can help."

"I'll do what I can for you," said Mr. Stokes, "but I don't s'pose your missis'll come to me at all. She saw you plain enough."

They walked on in silence and, still deep in thought over the matter, turned into a neighboring tavern for refreshment. Mr. Henshaw drank his with the air of a man performing a duty to his constitution; but Mr. Stokes, smacking his lips, waxed eloquent over the brew.

"I hardly know what I'm drinking," said his friend, forlornly. "I suppose it's four-half, because that's what I asked for."

Mr. Stokes gazed at him in deep sympathy. "It can't be so bad as that," he said, with concern.

"You wait till you're married," said Mr. Henshaw, brusquely. "You'd no business to ask me to go with you, and I was a good-natured fool to do it."

"You stick to your tale and it'll be all right," said the other. "Tell her that you spoke to me about it, and that his name is Alfred Bell—B E double L—and that he lives in—in Ireland. Here! I say!"

"Well," said Mr. Henshaw, shaking off the hand which the other had laid on his arm.

"You—you be Alfred Bell," said Mr. Stokes, breathlessly.

Mr. Henshaw started and eyed him nervously. His friend's eyes were bright and, he fancied, a bit wild.

"Be Alfred Bell," repeated Mr. Stokes. "Don't you see? Pretend to be Alfred Bell and go with me to your missis. I'll lend you a suit o' clothes and a fresh neck-tie, and there you are."

"What?" roared the astounded Mr. Henshaw.

"It's as easy as easy," declared the other. "Tomorrow evening, in a new rig-out, I walks you up to your house and asks for you to show you to yourself. Of course, I'm sorry you ain't in, and perhaps we walks in to wait for you."

"Show me to myself?" gasped Mr. Henshaw.

Mr. Stokes winked. "On account o' the surprising likeness," he said, smiling. "It is surprising, ain't it? Fancy the two of us sitting there and talking to her and waiting for you to come in and wondering what's making you so late!"

Mr. Henshaw regarded him steadfastly for some seconds, and then, taking a firm hold of his mug, slowly drained the contents.

"And what about my voice?" he demanded, with something approaching a sneer.

"That's right," said Mr. Stokes, hotly; "it wouldn't be you if you didn't try to make difficulties."

"But what about it?" said Mr. Henshaw, obstinately.

"You can alter it, can't you?" said the other.

They were alone in the bar, and Mr. Henshaw, after some persuasion, was induced to try a few experiments. He ranged from bass, which hurt his throat, to a falsetto which put Mr. Stokes's teeth on edge, but in vain. The rehearsal was stopped at last by the landlord, who, having twice come into the bar under the impression that fresh customers had entered, spoke his mind at some length. "Seem to think you're in a blessed monkey-house," he concluded, severely.

"We thought we was," said Mr. Stokes, with a long appraising sniff, as he opened the door. "It's a mistake anybody might make."

He pushed Mr. Henshaw into the street as the landlord placed a hand on the flap of the bar, and followed him out.

"You'll have to 'ave a bad cold and talk in 'usky whispers," he said slowly, as they walked along. "You caught a cold travelling in the train from Ireland day before yesterday, and you made it worse going for a ride on the outside of a 'bus with me and a couple o' ladies. See? Try 'usky whispers now."

Mr. Henshaw tried, and his friend, observing that he was taking but a languid interest in the scheme, was loud in his praises. "I should never 'ave known you," he declared. "Why, it's wonderful! Why didn't you tell me you could act like that?"

Mr. Henshaw remarked modestly that he had not been aware of it himself, and, taking a more hopeful view of the situation, whispered himself into such a state of hoarseness that another visit for refreshment became absolutely necessary.

"Keep your 'art up and practise," said Mr. Stokes, as he shook hands with him some time later. "And if you can manage it, get off at four o'clock to-morrow and we'll go round to see her while she thinks you're still at work."

Mr. Henshaw complimented him upon his artfulness, and, with some confidence in a man of such resource, walked home in a more cheerful frame of mind. His heart sank as he reached the house, but to his relief the lights were out and his wife was in bed.

He was up early next morning, but his wife showed no signs of rising. The cupboard was still empty, and for some time he moved about hungry and undecided. Finally he mounted the stairs again, and with a view to arranging matters for the evening remonstrated with her upon her behavior and loudly announced his intention of not coming home until she was in a better frame of mind. From a disciplinary point of view the effect of the remonstrance was somewhat lost by being shouted through the closed door, and he also broke off too abruptly when Mrs. Henshaw opened it suddenly and confronted him. Fragments of the peroration reached her through the front door.

Despite the fact that he left two hours earlier, the day passed but slowly, and he was in a very despondent state of mind by the time he reached Mr. Stokes's lodging. The latter, however, had cheerfulness enough for both, and, after helping his visitor to change into fresh clothes and part his hair in the middle instead of at the side, surveyed him with grinning satisfaction. Under his directions Mr. Henshaw also darkened his eyebrows and beard with a little burnt cork until Mr. Stokes declared that his own mother wouldn't know him.

"Now, be careful," said Mr. Stokes, as they set off. "Be bright and cheerful; be a sort o' ladies' man to her, same as she saw you with the one on the 'bus. Be as unlike yourself as you can, and don't forget yourself and call her by 'er pet name."

"Pet name!" said Mr. Henshaw, indignantly. "Pet name! You'll alter your ideas of married life when you're caught, my lad, I can tell you!"

He walked on in scornful silence, lagging farther and farther behind as they neared his house. When Mr. Stokes knocked at the door he stood modestly aside with his back against the wall of the next house.

"Is George in?" inquired Mr. Stokes, carelessly, as Mrs. Henshaw opened the door.

"No," was the reply.

Mr. Stokes affected to ponder; Mr. Henshaw instinctively edged away.

"He ain't in," said Mrs. Henshaw, preparing to close the door.

"I wanted to see 'im partikler," said Mr. Stokes, slowly. "I brought a friend o' mine, name o' Alfred Bell, up here on purpose to see 'im."

Mrs. Henshaw, following the direction of his eyes, put her head round the door.

"George!" she exclaimed, sharply.

Mr. Stokes smiled. "That ain't George," he said, gleefully; "That's my friend, Mr. Alfred Bell. Ain't it a extraordinary likeness? Ain't it wonderful? That's why I brought 'im up; I wanted George to see 'im."

Mrs. Henshaw looked from one to the other in wrathful bewilderment.

"His living image, ain't he?" said Mr. Stokes. "This is my pal George's missis," he added, turning to Mr. Bell.

"Good afternoon to you," said that gentleman, huskily.

"He got a bad cold coming from Ireland," explained Mr. Stokes, "and, foolish-like, he went outside a 'bus with me the other night and made it worse."

"Oh-h!" said Mrs. Henshaw, slowly. "Indeed! Really!"

"He's quite curious to see George," said Mr. Stokes. "In fact, he was going back to Ireland tonight if it 'adn't been for that. He's waiting till to-morrow just to see George."

Mr. Bell, in a voice huskier than ever, said that he had altered his mind again.

"Nonsense!" said Mr. Stokes, sternly. "Besides, George would like to see you. I s'pose he won't be long?" he added, turning to Mrs. Henshaw, who was regarding Mr. Bell much as a hungry cat regards a plump sparrow.

"I don't suppose so," she said, slowly.

"I dare say if we wait a little while—" began Mr. Stokes, ignoring a frantic glance from Mr. Henshaw.

"Come in," said Mrs. Henshaw, suddenly.

Mr. Stokes entered and, finding that his friend hung back, went out again and half led, half pushed him indoors. Mr. Bell's shyness he attributed to his having lived so long in Ireland.

"He is quite the ladies' man, though," he said, artfully, as they followed their hostess into the front room. "You should ha' seen 'im the other night on the 'bus. We had a couple o' lady friends o' mine with us, and even the conductor was surprised at his goings on."

Mr. Bell, by no means easy as to the results of the experiment, scowled at him despairingly.

"Carrying on, was he?" said Mrs. Henshaw, regarding the culprit steadily.

"Carrying on like one o'clock," said the imaginative Mr. Stokes. "Called one of 'em his little wife, and asked her where 'er wedding-ring was."

"I didn't," said Mr. Bell, in a suffocating voice. "I didn't."

"There's nothing to be ashamed of," said Mr. Stokes, virtuously. "Only, as I said to you at the time, 'Alfred,' I says, 'it's all right for you as a single man, but you might be the twin-brother of a pal o' mine— George Henshaw by name—and if some people was to see you they might think it was 'im.' Didn't I say that?"

"You did," said Mr. Bell, helplessly.

"And he wouldn't believe me," said Mr. Stokes, turning to Mrs. Henshaw. "That's why I brought him round to see George."

"I should like to see the two of 'em together myself," said Mrs. Henshaw, quietly. "I should have taken him for my husband anywhere."

"You wouldn't if you'd seen 'im last night," said Mr. Stokes, shaking his head and smiling.

"Carrying on again, was he?" inquired Mrs. Henshaw, quickly.

"No!" said Mr. Bell, in a stentorian whisper.

His glance was so fierce that Mr. Stokes almost quailed. "I won't tell tales out of school," he said, nodding.

"Not if I ask you to?" said Mrs. Henshaw, with a winning smile.

"Ask 'im," said Mr. Stokes.

"Last night," said the whisperer, hastily, "I went for a quiet walk round Victoria Park all by myself. Then I met Mr. Stokes, and we had one half-pint together at a public-house. That's all."

Mrs. Henshaw looked at Mr. Stokes. Mr. Stokes winked at her.

"It's as true as my name is—Alfred Bell," said that gentleman, with slight but natural hesitation.

"Have it your own way," said Mr. Stokes, somewhat perturbed at Mr. Bell's refusal to live up to the character he had arranged for him.

"I wish my husband spent his evenings in the same quiet way," said Mrs. Henshaw, shaking her head.

"Don't he?" said Mr. Stokes. "Why, he always seems quiet enough to me. Too quiet, I should say. Why, I never knew a quieter man. I chaff 'im about it sometimes."

"That's his artfulness," said Mrs. Henshaw.

"Always in a hurry to get 'ome," pursued the benevolent Mr. Stokes.

"He may say so to you to get away from you," said Mrs. Henshaw, thoughtfully. "He does say you're hard to shake off sometimes."

Mr. Stokes sat stiffly upright and threw a fierce glance in the direction of Mr. Henshaw.

"Pity he didn't tell me," he said bitterly. "I ain't one to force my company where it ain't wanted."

"I've said to him sometimes," continued Mrs. Henshaw, "'Why don't you tell Ted Stokes plain that you don't like his company?' but he won't. That ain't his way. He'd sooner talk of you behind your back."

"What does he say?" inquired Mr. Stokes, coldly ignoring a frantic headshake on the part of his friend.

"Promise me you won't tell him if I tell you," said Mrs. Henshaw.

Mr. Stokes promised.

"I don't know that I ought to tell you," said Mrs. Henshaw, reluctantly, "but I get so sick and tired of him coming home and grumbling about you."

"Go on," said the waiting Stokes.

Mrs. Henshaw stole a glance at him. "He says you act as if you thought yourself everybody," she said, softly, "and your everlasting clack, clack, clack, worries him to death."

"Go on," said the listener, grimly.

"And he says it's so much trouble to get you to pay for your share of the drinks that he'd sooner pay himself and have done with it."

Mr. Stokes sprang from his chair and, with clenched fists, stood angrily regarding the horrified Mr. Bell. He composed himself by an effort and resumed his seat.

"Anything else?" he inquired.

"Heaps and heaps of things," said Mrs. Henshaw; "but I don't want to make bad blood between you."

"Don't mind me," said Mr. Stokes, glancing balefully over at his agitated friend. "P'raps I'll tell you some things about him some day."

"It would be only fair," said Mrs. Henshaw, quickly. "Tell me now; I don't mind Mr. Bell hearing; not a bit."

Mr. Bell spoke up for himself. "I don't want to hear family secrets," he whispered, with an imploring glance at the vindictive Mr. Stokes. "It wouldn't be right."

"Well, I don't want to say things behind a man's back," said the latter, recovering himself. "Let's wait till George comes in, and I'll say 'em before his face."

Mrs. Henshaw, biting her lip with annoyance, argued with him, but in vain. Mr. Stokes was firm, and, with a glance at the clock, said that George would be in soon and he would wait till he came.

Conversation flagged despite the efforts of Mrs. Henshaw to draw Mr. Bell out on the subject of Ireland At an early stage of the catechism he lost his voice entirely, and thereafter sat silent while Mrs. Henshaw discussed the most intimate affairs of her husband's family with Mr. Stokes. She was in the middle of an anecdote about her mother-in-law when Mr. Bell rose and, with some difficulty, intimated his desire to depart.

"What, without seeing George?" said Mrs. Henshaw. "He can't be long now, and I should like to see you together."

"P'r'aps we shall meet him," said Mr. Stokes, who was getting rather tired of the affair. "Good night."

He led the way to the door and, followed by the eager Mr. Bell, passed out into the street. The knowledge that Mrs. Henshaw was watching him from the door kept him silent until they had turned the corner, and then, turning fiercely on Mr. Henshaw, he demanded to know what he meant by it.

"I've done with you," he said, waving aside the other's denials. "I've got you out of this mess, and now I've done with you. It's no good talking, because I don't want to hear it."

"Good-by, then," said Mr. Henshaw, with unexpected hauteur, as he came to a standstill.

"I'll 'ave my trousers first, though," said Mr. Stokes, coldly, "and then you can go, and welcome."

"It's my opinion she recognized me, and said all that just to try us," said the other, gloomily.

Mr. Stokes scorned to reply, and reaching his lodging stood by in silence while the other changed his clothes. He refused Mr. Henshaw's hand with a gesture he had once seen on the stage, and, showing him downstairs, closed the door behind him with a bang.

Left to himself, the small remnants of Mr. Henshaw's courage disappeared. He wandered forlornly up and down the streets until past ten o'clock, and then, cold and dispirited, set off in the direction of home. At the corner of the street he pulled himself together by a great effort, and walking rapidly to his house put the key in the lock and turned it.

The door was fast and the lights were out. He knocked, at first lightly, but gradually increasing in loudness. At the fourth knock a light appeared in the room above, the window was raised, and Mrs. Henshaw leaned out

"Mr. Bell!" she said, in tones of severe surprise.

"Bell?" said her husband, in a more surprised voice still. "It's me, Polly."

"Go away at once, sir!" said Mrs. Henshaw, indignantly. "How dare you call me by my Christian name? I'm surprised at you!"

"It's me, I tell you—George!" said her husband, desperately. "What do you mean by calling me Bell?"

"If you're Mr. Bell, as I suppose, you know well enough," said Mrs. Henshaw, leaning out and regarding him fixedly; "and if you're George you don't."

"I'm George," said Mr. Henshaw, hastily.

"I'm sure I don't know what to make of it," said Mrs. Henshaw, with a bewildered air. "Ted Stokes brought round a man named Bell this afternoon so like you that I can't tell the difference. I don't know what to do, but I do know this—I don't let you in until I have seen you both together, so that I can tell which is which."

"Both together!" exclaimed the startled Mr. Henshaw. "Here—look here!"

He struck a match and, holding it before his face, looked up at the window. Mrs. Henshaw scrutinized him gravely.

"It's no good," she said, despairingly. "I can't tell. I must see you both together."

Mr. Henshaw ground his teeth. "But where is he?" he inquired.

"He went off with Ted Stokes," said his wife. "If you're George you'd better go and ask him."

She prepared to close the window, but Mr. Henshaw's voice arrested her.

"And suppose he is not there?" he said.

Mrs. Henshaw reflected. "If he is not there bring Ted Stokes back with you," she said at last, "and if he says you're George, I'll let you in." The window closed and the light disappeared. Mr. Henshaw waited for some time, but in vain, and, with a very clear idea of the reception he would meet with at the hands of Mr. Stokes, set off to his lodging.

If anything, he had underestimated his friend's powers. Mr. Stokes, rudely disturbed just as he had got into bed, was the incarnation of wrath. He was violent, bitter, and insulting in a breath, but Mr. Henshaw was desperate, and Mr. Stokes, after vowing over and over again that nothing should induce him to accompany him back to his house, was at last so moved by his entreaties that he went upstairs and equipped himself for the journey.

"And, mind, after this I never want to see your face again," he said, as they walked swiftly back.

Mr. Henshaw made no reply. The events of the day had almost exhausted him, and silence was maintained until they reached the house. Much to his relief he heard somebody moving about upstairs after the first knock, and in a very short time the window was gently raised and Mrs.

Henshaw looked out.

"What, you've come back?" she said, in a low, intense voice. "Well, of all the impudence! How dare you carry on like this?"

"It's me," said her husband.

"Yes, I see it is," was the reply.

"It's him right enough; it's your husband," said Mr. Stokes. "Alfred Bell has gone."

"How dare you stand there and tell me them falsehoods!" exclaimed Mrs. Henshaw. "I wonder the ground don't open and swallow you up. It's Mr. Bell, and if he don't go away I'll call the police."

Messrs. Henshaw and Stokes, amazed at their reception, stood blinking up at her. Then they conferred in whispers.

"If you can't tell 'em apart, how do you know this is Mr. Bell?" inquired Mr. Stokes, turning to the window again.

"How do I know?" repeated Mrs. Henshaw. "How do I know? Why, because my husband came home almost directly Mr. Bell had gone. I wonder he didn't meet him."

"Came home?" cried Mr. Henshaw, shrilly. "Came home?"

"Yes; and don't make so much noise," said Mrs. Henshaw, tartly; "he's asleep."

The two gentlemen turned and gazed at each other in stupefaction. Mr. Stokes was the first to recover, and, taking his dazed friend by the arm, led him gently away. At the end of the street he took a deep breath, and, after a slight pause to collect his scattered energies, summed up the situation.

"She's twigged it all along," he said, with conviction. "You'll have to come home with me tonight, and to-morrow the best thing you can do is to make a clean breast of it. It was a silly game, and, if you remember, I was against it from the first."

"CHOICE SPIRITS"

The day was fine, and the breeze so light that the old patched sails were taking the schooner along at a gentle three knots per hour. A sail or two shone like snow in the offing, and a gull hovered in the air astern. From the cabin to the galley, and from the galley to the untidy tangle in the bows, there was no sign of anybody to benefit by the conversation of the skipper and mate as they discussed a wicked and mutinous spirit which had become observable in the crew.

"It's sheer rank wickedness, that's what it is," said the skipper, a small elderly man, with grizzled beard and light blue eyes.

"Rank," agreed the mate, whose temperament was laconic.

"Why, when I was a boy you wouldn't believe what I had to eat," said the skipper; "not if I took my Bible oath on it, you wouldn't."

"They're dainty," said the mate.

"Dainty!" said the other indignantly. "What right have hungry sailormen to be dainty? Don't I give them enough to eat? Look! Look there!"

He drew back, choking, and pointed with his forefinger as Bill Smith, A.B., came on deck with a plate held at arm's length, and a nose disdainfully elevated. He affected not to see the skipper, and, walking in a mincing fashion to the side, raked the food from the plate into the sea with his fingers. He was followed by George Simpson, A.B., who in the same objectionable fashion wasted food which the skipper had intended should nourish his frame.

"I'll pay 'em for this!" murmured the skipper.

"There's some more," said the mate.

Two more men came on deck, grinning consciously, and disposed of their dinners. Then there was an interval—an interval in which everybody, fore and aft, appeared to be waiting for something; the something being at that precise moment standing at the foot of the foc'sle ladder, trying to screw its courage up.

"If the boy comes," said the skipper in a strained, unnatural voice, "I'll flay him alive."

"You'd better get your knife out then," said the mate.

The boy appeared on deck, very white about the gills, and looking piteously at the crew for support. He became conscious from their scowls that he had forgotten something, and remembering himself, stretched out his skinny arms to their full extent, and, crinkling his nose, walked with great trepidation to the side.

"Boy!" vociferated the skipper suddenly.

"Yessir," said the urchin hastily.

"Comm'ere," said the skipper sternly.

"Shove your dinner over first," said four low, menacing voices.

The boy hesitated, then walked slowly towards the skipper.

"What are you going to do with that dinner?" demanded the latter grimly.

"Eat it," said the youth modestly.

"What d'yer bring it on deck for, then?" inquired the other, bending his brows on him.

"I thought it would taste better on deck, sir," said the boy.

"Taste better!" growled the skipper ferociously. "Ain't it good?"

"Yessir," said the boy.

"Speak louder," said the skipper sternly. "Is it very good?"

"Beautiful," said the boy in a shrill falsetto.

"Did you ever taste better wittles than you get aboard this ship?" demanded the skipper, setting him a fine example in loud speaking.

"Never," yelled the boy, following it.

"Everything as it should be?" roared the skipper.

"Better than it should be," shrilled the craven.

"Sit down and eat it," commanded the other.

The boy sat on the cabin skylight, and, taking out his pocket-knife, began his meal with every appearance of enjoyment, the skipper, with his elbows on the side, and his legs crossed, regarding him serenely.

"I suppose," he said loudly, after watching the boy for some time, "I s'pose the men threw theirs overboard becos they hadn't been used to such good food?"

"Yessir," said the boy.

"Did they say so?" bawled the other.

The boy hesitated, and glanced nervously forward. "Yessir," he said at length, and shuddered as a low, ominous growl came from the crew. Despite his slowness, the meal came to an end at last, and, in obedience to orders, he rose, and taking his plate forward, looked entreatingly at the crew as he passed them.

"Come down below," said Bill; "we want to have a talk with you."

"Can't," said the boy. "I've got my work to do. I haven't got time to talk."

He stayed up on deck until evening, and then, the men's anger having evaporated somewhat, crept softly below, and climbed into his bunk. Simpson leaned over and made a clutch at him, but Bill pushed him aside.

"Leave him alone," said he quietly; "we'll take it out of him to-morrow."

For some time Tommy lay worrying over the fate in store for him, and then, yielding to fatigue, turned over and slept soundly until he was awakened some three hours later by the men's voices, and, looking out, saw that the lamp was alight and the crew at supper, listening quietly to Bill, who was speaking.

"I've a good mind to strike, that's what I've a good mind to do," he said savagely, as, after an attempt at the butter, he put it aside and ate dry biscuit.

"An' get six months," said old Ned. "That won't do, Bill."

"Are we to go a matter of six or seven days on dry biscuit and rotten taters?" demanded the other fiercely. "Why, it's slow sooicide."

"I wish one of you would commit sooicide," said Ned, looking wistfully round at the faces, "that 'ud frighten the old man, and bring him round a bit."

"Well, you're the eldest," said Bill pointedly.

"Drowning's a easy death too," said Simpson persuasively. "You can't have much enjoyment in life at your age, Ned?"

"And you might leave a letter behind to the skipper, saying as 'ow you was drove to it by bad food," said the cook, who was getting excited.

"Talk sense!" said the old man very shortly.

"Look here," said Bill suddenly. "I tell you what we can do: let one of us pretend to commit suicide, and write a letter as Slushy here ses, saying as 'ow we're gone overboard sooner than be starved to death. It 'ud scare the old man proper; and p'raps he'd let us start on the other meat without eating up this rotten stuff first."

"How's it to be done?" asked Simpson, staring.

"Go an' 'ide down the fore 'old," said Bill. "There's not much stuff down there. We'll take off the hatch when one of us is on watch to-night, and—whoever wants to—can go and hide down there till the old man's come to his senses. What do you think of it, mates?"

"It's all right as an idea," said Ned slowly, "but who's going?"

"Tommy," replied Bill simply.

"Blest if I ever thought of him," said Ned admiringly; "did you, cookie?"

"Never crossed my mind," said the cook.

"You see the best o' Tommy's going," said Bill, "is that the old man 'ud only give him a flogging if he found it out. We wouldn't split as to who put the hatch on over him. He can be there as comfortable as you please, do nothing, and sleep all day if he likes. O' course we don't know anything about it, we miss Tommy, and find the letter wrote on this table."

The cook leaned forward and regarded his colleague favourably; then he pursed his lips, and nodded significantly at an upper bunk from which the face of Tommy, pale and scared, looked anxiously down.

"Halloa!" said Bill, "have you heard what we've been saying?"

"I heard you say something about going to drown old Ned," said Tommy guardedly.

"He's heard all about it," said the cook severely. "Do you know where little boys who tell lies go to, Tommy?"

"I'd sooner go there than down the fore 'old," said Tommy, beginning to knuckle his eyes. "I won't go. I'll tell the skipper."

"No you won't," said Bill sternly. "This is your punishment for them lies you told about us to-day, an' very cheap you've got off too. Now, get out o' that bunk. Come on afore I pull you out."

With a miserable whimper the youth dived beneath his blankets, and, clinging frantically to the edge of his berth, kicked convulsively as he was lifted down, blankets and all, and accommodated with a seat at the table.

"Pen and ink and paper, Ned," said Bill.

The old man produced them, and Bill, first wiping off with his coat-sleeve a piece of butter which the paper had obtained from the table, spread it before the victim.

"I can't write," said Tommy suddenly.

The men looked at each other in dismay.

"It's a lie," said the cook.

"I tell you I can't," said the urchin, becoming hopeful; "that's why they sent me to sea, becos I couldn't read or write."

"Pull his ear, Bill," said Ned, annoyed at these aspersions upon an honourable profession.

"It don't matter," said Bill calmly. "I'll write it for 'im; the old man don't know my fist."

He sat down at the table, and, squaring his shoulders, took a noisy dip of ink, and scratching his head, looked pensively at the paper.

"Better spell it bad, Bill," suggested Ned.

"Ay, ay," said the other. "'Ow do you think a boy would spell 'sooicide,' Ned?"

The old man pondered. "S-o-o-e-y-s-i-d-e," he said slowly.

"Why, that's the right way, ain't it?" inquired the cook, looking from one to the other.

"We mustn't spell it right," said Bill, with his pen hovering over the paper. "Be careful, Ned."

"We'll say 'killed myself instead,'" said the old man. "A boy wouldn't use such a big word as that p'raps."

Bill bent over his work, and, apparently paying great attention to his friends' entreaties not to write it too well, slowly wrote the letter.

"How's this?" he inquired, sitting back in his seat.

"'Deer captin i take my pen in hand for the larst time to innform you that i am no more suner than heat the 'orrible stuff what you kail meet i have drownded miself it is a moor easy death than starvin' i 'ave left my clasp nife to bill an' my silver wotch to it is 'ard too dee so young tommie brown.'"

"Splendid!" said Ned, as the reader finished and looked inquiringly round.

"I put in that bit about the knife and the watch to make it seem real," said Bill, with modest pride; "but, if you like, I'll leave 'em to you instead, Ned."

"I don't want 'em," said the old man generously.

"Put your cloes on," said Bill, turning to the whimpering Tommy.

"I'm not going down that fore 'old," said Tommy desperately. "You may as well know now as later on—I won't go."

"Cookie," said Bill calmly, "just 'and me them cloes, will you? Now, Tommy."

"I tell you I'm not going to," said Tommy.

"An' that little bit o' rope, cookie," said Bill; "it's just down by your 'and. Now, Tommy."

The youngest member of the crew looked from his clothes to the rope, and from the rope back to his clothes again.

"How 'm I goin' to be fed?" he demanded sullenly, as he began to dress.

"You'll have a stone bottle o' water to take down with you an' some biskits," replied Bill, "an' of a night-time we'll hand you down some o' that meat you're so fond of. Hide 'em behind the cargo, an' if you hear anybody take the hatch off in the daytime, nip behind it yourself."

"An' what about fresh air?" demanded the sacrifice.

"You'll 'ave fresh air of a night when the hatch is took off," said Bill. "Don't you worry, I've thought of everything."

The arrangements being concluded, they waited until Simpson relieved the mate at the helm, and then trooped up on deck, half pushing and half leading their reluctant victim.

"It's just as if he was going on a picnic," said old Ned, as the boy stood unwillingly on the deck, with a stone bottle in one hand and some biscuits wrapped up in an old newspaper in the other.

"Lend a 'and, Bill. Easy does it."

Noiselessly the two seamen took off the hatch, and, as Tommy declined to help in the proceedings at all, Ned clambered down first to receive him. Bill took him by the scruff of the neck and lowered him, kicking strongly, into the hold.

"Have you got him?" he inquired.

"Yes," said Ned in a smothered voice, and, depositing the boy in the hold, hastily clambered up again, wiping his mouth.

"Been having a swig at the bottle?" inquired Bill.

"Boy's heel," said Ned very shortly. "Get the hatch on."

The hatch was replaced, and Bill and his fellow conspirator, treading quietly and not without some apprehension for the morrow, went below and turned in. Tommy, who had been at sea long enough to take things as he found them, curled up in the corner of the hold, and with his bottle as a pillow fell asleep.

It was not until eight o'clock next morning that the master of the Sunbeam discovered that he was a boy short. He questioned the cook as he sat at breakfast The cook, who was a very nervous man, turned pale, set the coffee-pot down with a thump which upset some of the liquor, and bolted up on deck. The skipper, after shouting for him in some of the most alluring swear words known on the high seas, went raging up on deck, where he found the men standing in a little knot, looking very ill at ease.

"Bill," said the skipper uneasily, "what's the matter with that damned cook?"

"'E's 'ad a shock, sir," said Bill, shaking his head; "we've all 'ad a shock."

"You'll have another in a minute," said the skipper emotionally. "Where's the boy?"

For a moment Bill's hardihood forsook him, and he looked helplessly at his mates. In their anxiety to avoid his gaze they looked over the side, and a horrible fear came over the skipper. He looked at Bill mutely, and Bill held out a dirty piece of paper.

The skipper read it through in a state of stupefaction, then he handed it to the mate, who had followed him on deck. The mate read it and handed it back.

"It's yours," he said shortly.

"I don't understand it," said the skipper, shaking his head. "Why, only yesterday he was up on deck here eating his dinner, and saying it was the best meat he ever tasted. You heard him, Bob?"

"I heard him, pore little devil!" said the mate.

"You all heard him," said the skipper. "Well, there's five witnesses I've got. He must have been mad. Didn't nobody hear him go overboard?"

"I 'eard a splash, sir, in my watch," said Bill.

"Why didn't you run and see what it was?" demanded the other.

"I thought it was one of the chaps come up to throw his supper overboard," said Bill simply.

"Ah!" said the skipper, biting his lip, "did you? You're always going on about the grub. What's the matter with it?"

"It's pizon, sir," said Ned, shaking his head. "The meat's awful."

"It's as sweet as nuts," said the skipper. "Well, you can have it out of the other tank if you like. Will that satisfy you?"

The men brightened up a little and nudged each other.

"The butter's bad too, sir," said Bill.

"Butter bad!" said the skipper, frowning. "How's that, cook?"

"I ain't done nothing to it, sir," said the cook helplessly.

"Give 'em butter out o' the firkin in the cabin," growled the skipper. "It's my firm belief you'd been ill-using that boy; the food was delicious."

He walked off, taking the letter with him, and, propping it up against the sugar-basin, made but a poor breakfast.

For that day the men lived, as Ned put it, on the fat of the land, in addition to the other luxuries. Figgy duff, a luxury hitherto reserved for Sundays, being also served out to them. Bill was regarded as a big-brained benefactor of the human race; joy reigned in the foc'sle, and at night the hatch was taken off and the prisoner regaled with a portion which had been saved for him. He ate it ungratefully, and put churlish and inconvenient questions as to what was to happen at the end of the voyage.

"Well smuggle you ashore all right," said Bill; "none of us are going to sign back in this old tub. I'll take you aboard some ship with me—Eh?"

"I didn't say anything," said Tommy untruthfully.

To the wrath and confusion of the crew, next day their commanding officer put them back on the old diet again. The old meat was again served out, and the grass-fed luxury from the cabin stopped. Bill shared the fate of all leaders when things go wrong, and, from being the idol of his fellows, became a butt for their gibes.

"What about your little idea now?" grunted old Ned, scornfully, that evening as he broke his biscuit roughly with his teeth, and dropped it into his basin of tea.

"You ain't as clever as you thought you was, Bill," said the cook with the air of a discoverer.

"And there's that pore dear boy shut up in the dark for nothing," said Simpson, with somewhat belated thoughtfulness. "An' cookie doing his work."

"I'm not going to be beat," said Bill blackly; "the old man was badly scared yesterday. We must have another sooicide, that's all."

"Let Tommy do it again," suggested the cook flippantly, and they all laughed.

"Two on one trip 'll about do the old man up," said Bill, regarding the interruption unfavourably. "Now, who's going to be the next?"

"We've had enough o' this game," said Simpson, shrugging his shoulders; "you've gone cranky, Bill."

"No I ain't," said Bill; "I'm not going to be beat, that's all. Whoever goes down, they'll have a nice, easy, lazy time. Sleep all day if he likes, and nothing to do. You ain't been looking very well lately, Ned."

"Oh?" said the old man coldly.

"Well, settle it between you," said Bill carelessly; "it's all one to me, which of you goes."

"Ho, an' what about you?" demanded Simpson.

"Me?" inquired Bill in astonishment. "Why, I've got to stay up here and manage it."

"Well, we'll stay up and help you," said Simpson derisively.

Ned and the cook laughed, Simpson joined in. Bill rose, and, going to his bunk, fished out a pack of greasy cards from beneath his bedding.

"Larst cut, sooicide," he said briefly, "I'm in it."

He held the pack before the cook. The cook hesitated, and looked at the other two.

"Don't be a fool, Bill," said Simpson.

"Why, do you funk it?" sneered Bill.

"It's a fool's game, I tell you," said Simpson.

"Well, you 'elped me start it," said the other. "You're afraid, that's what you are,—afraid. You can let the boy go down there, but when it comes to yourselves you turn chicken-'arted."

"All right," said Simpson recklessly, "let Bill 'ave 'is way; cut, cookie."

Sorely against his will the cook complied, and drew a ten; Ned, after much argument, cut and drew seven; Simpson, with a king in his fist, leaned back on the locker and fingered his beard nonchalantly. "Go on, Bill," he said; "see what you can do."

Bill took the pack and shuffled it "I orter be able to beat seven," he said slowly. He handed the pack to Ned, drew a card, and the other three sat back and laughed boisterously.

"Three!" said Simpson. "Bravo, Bill! I'll write your letter for you; he'd know your writing. What shall I say?"

"Say what you like," retorted Bill, breathing hard as he thought of the hold.

He sat back sneering disdainfully, as the other three merrily sat down to compose his letter, replying only by a contemptuous silence when Simpson asked him whether he wanted any kisses put in. When the letter was handed over for his inspection he only made one remark.

"I thought you could write better than that, George," he said haughtily.

"I'm writing it for you," said Simpson.

Bill's hauteur vanished and he became his old self again. "If you want a plug in the eye, George," he said feelingly, "you've only got to say so, you know."

His temper was so unpleasant that half the pleasure of the evening was spoiled, and instead of being conducted to his hiding-place with quips and light laughter, the proceedings were more like a funeral than anything else. The crowning touch to his ill-nature was furnished by Tommy, who upon coming up and learning that Bill was to be his room-mate, gave way to a fit of the most unfeigned horror.

"There's another letter for you this morning," said the mate, as the skipper came out of his stateroom buttoning up his waistcoat.

"Another what?" demanded the other, turning pale.

The mate jerked his thumb upwards. "Old Ned has got it," he continued. "I can't think what's come over the men."

The skipper dashed up on deck, and mechanically took the letter from Ned and read it through. He stood for some time like a man in a dream, and then stumbled down the forecastle, and looked in all the bunks and even under the table; then he came up and stood by the hold, with his head on one side. The men held their breath.

"What's the meaning of all this?" he demanded at length, sitting limply on the hatch, with his eyes down.

"Bad grub, sir," said Simpson, gaining courage from his manner; "that's what we'll have to say when we get ashore."

"You're not to say a word about it!" said the other, firing up.

"It's our dooty, sir," said Ned impressively.

"Look here now," said the skipper, and he looked at the remaining members of the crew entreatingly. "Don't let's have no more suicides. The old meat's gone now, and you can start the other, and when we get to port I'll ship in some fresh butter and vegetables. But I don't want you to say anything about the food being bad, or about these letters, when we get to port I shall simply say the two of 'em disappeared, an' I want you to say the same."

"It can't be done, sir," said Simpson firmly.

The skipper rose and walked to the side. "Would a fi'pun note make any difference?" he asked in a low voice.

"It 'ud make a little difference," said Ned cautiously.

The skipper looked up at Simpson. On the face of Simpson was an expression of virtuous arithmetical determination.

The skipper looked down again. "Or a fi'pun note each?" he said, in a low voice. "I can't go beyond that."

"Call it twenty pun and it's a bargain, ain't it, mates?" said Simpson.

Ned said it was, and even the cook forgot his nervousness, and said it was evident the skipper meant to do the generous thing, and they'd stand by him.

"Where's the money coming from?" inquired the mate, as the skipper went down to breakfast, and discussed the matter with him. "They wouldn't get nothing out of me!"

The skylight was open; the skipper with a glance at it bent forward and whispered in his ear.

"Wot!" said the mate. He endeavoured to suppress his laughter with hot coffee and bacon, with the result that he had to rise from his seat and stand patiently while the skipper dealt him some hearty thumps on the back.

With the prospect of riches before them the men cheerfully faced the extra work; the cook did the boy's, while Ned and Simpson did Bill's between them. When night came they removed the hatch again, and with a little curiosity waited to hear how their victims were progressing.

"Where's my dinner?" growled Bill hungrily, as he drew himself up on deck.

"Dinner!" said Ned, in surprise; "why, you ain't got none."

"Wot?" said Bill ferociously.

"You see the skipper only serves out for three now," said the cook.

"Well, why didn't you save us some?" demanded the other.

"There ain't enough of it, Bill, there ain't indeed," said Ned. "We have to do more work now, and there ain't enough even for us. You've got biscuit and water, haven't you?"

Bill swore at him.

"I've 'ad enough o' this," he said fiercely. "I'm coming up, let the old man do what he likes. I don't care."

"Don't do that, Bill," said the old man persuasively. "Everything's going beautiful. You was quite right what you said about the old man. We was wrong. He's skeered fearful, and he's going to give us twenty pun to say nothing about it when we get ashore."

"I'm going to have ten out o' that," said Bill, brightening a little, "and it's worth it too. I get the 'orrors shut up down there all day."

"Ay, ay," said Ned, with a side kick at the cook, who was about to question Bill's method of division.

"The old man sucked it all in beautiful," said the cook. "He's in a dreadful way. He's got all your clothes and things, and the boy's, and he's going to 'and 'em over to your friends. It's the best joke I ever heard."

"You're a fool!" said Bill shortly, and lighting his pipe went and squatted in the bows to wrestle grimly with a naturally bad temper.

For the ensuing four days things went on smoothly enough. The weather being fair, the watch at night was kept by the men, and regularly they had to go through the unpleasant Jack-in-the-box experience of taking the lid off Bill. The sudden way he used to pop out and rate them about his sufferings and their callousness was extremely trying, and it was only by much persuasion and reminders of his share of the hush-money that they could persuade him to return again to his lair at daybreak.

Still undisturbed they rounded the Land's End. The day had been close and muggy, but towards night the wind freshened, and the schooner began to slip at a good pace through the water. The two prisoners, glad to escape from the stifling atmosphere of the hold, sat in the bows with an appetite which the air made only too keen for the preparations made to satisfy it.

Ned was steering, and the other two men having gone below and turned in, there were no listeners to their low complaints about the food.

"It's a fool's game, Tommy," said Bill, shaking his head.

"Game?" said Tommy, sniffing. "'Ow are we going to get away when we get to Northsea?"

"You leave that to me," said Bill. "Old Ned seems to ha' got a bad cough," he added.

"He's choking, I should think," said Tommy, leaning forward. "Look! he's waving his hand at us."

Both sprang up hastily, but ere they could make any attempt to escape the skipper and mate emerged from the companion and walked towards them.

"Look here," said the skipper, turning to the mate, and indicating the culprits with his hand; "perhaps you'll disbelieve in dreams now."

"'Straordinary!" said the mate, rubbing his eyes, as Bill stood sullenly waiting events, while the miserable Tommy skulked behind him.

"I've heard o' such things," continued the skipper, in impressive tones, "but I never expected to see it You can't say you haven't seen a ghost now, Bob."

"'Straordinary!" said the mate, shaking his head again. "Lifelike!"

"The ship's haunted, Ned," cried the skipper in hollow tones. "Here's the sperrits o' Bill and the boy standing agin the windlass."

The bewildered old seaman made no reply; the smaller spirit sniffed and wiped his nose on his cuff, and the larger one began to whistle softly.

"Poor things!" said the skipper, after they had discussed these extraordinary apparitions for some time. "Can you see the windlass through the boy, Bob?"

"I can see through both of 'em," said the mate slyly.

They stayed on deck a little longer, and then coming to the conclusion that their presence on deck could do no good, and indeed seemed only to embarrass their visitors, went below again, leaving all hands a prey to the wildest astonishment.

"Wot's 'is little game?" asked Simpson, coming cautiously up on deck.

"Damned if I know," said Bill savagely.

"He don't really think you're ghosts?" suggested the cook feebly.

"O' course not," said Bill scornfully. "He's got some little game on. Well, I'm going to my bunk. You'd better come too, Tommy. We'll find out what it all means to-morrer, I've no doubt."

On the morrow they received a little enlightenment, for after breakfast the cook came forward nervously to break the news that meat and vegetables had only been served out for three. Consternation fell upon all.

"I'll go an' see 'im," said Bill ravenously.

He found the skipper laughing heartily over something with the mate. At the seaman's approach he stepped back and eyed him coolly.

"Mornin', sir," said Bill, shuffling up. "We'd like to know, sir, me an' Tommy, whether we can have our rations for dinner served out now same as before?"

"Dinner?" said the skipper in surprise. "What do you want dinner for?"

"Eat," said Bill, eyeing him reproachfully.

"Eat?" said the skipper. "What's the good o' giving dinner to a ghost? Why you've got nowhere to put it."

By dint of great self-control Bill smiled in a ghastly fashion, and patted his stomach.

"All air," said the skipper turning away.

"Can we have our clothes and things then?" said Bill grinding his teeth. "Ned says as how you've got 'em."

"Certainly not," said the skipper. "I take 'em home and give 'em to your next o' kin. That's the law, ain't it, Bob?"

"It is," said the mate.

"They'll 'ave your effects and your pay up to the night you committed suicide," said the skipper.

"We didn't commit sooicide," said Bill; "how could we when we're standing here?"

"Oh, yes, you did," said the other. "I've got your letters in my pocket to prove it; besides, if you didn't I should give you in charge for desertion directly we get to port."

He exchanged glances with the mate, and Bill, after standing first on one leg and then on the other, walked slowly away. For the rest of the morning he stayed below setting the smaller ghost a bad example in the way of language, and threatening his fellows with all sorts of fearful punishments.

Until dinner-time the skipper heard no more of them, but he had just finished that meal and lit his pipe when he heard footsteps on the deck, and the next moment old Ned, hot and angry, burst into the cabin.

"Bill's stole our dinner, sir," he panted unceremoniously.

"Who?" inquired the skipper coldly.

"Bill, sir, Bill Smith," replied Ned.

"Who?" inquired the skipper more coldly than before.

"The ghost o' Bill Smith," growled Ned, correcting himself savagely, "has took our dinner away, an' him an' the ghost o' Tommy Brown is a sitting down and boltin' of it as fast as they can bolt."

"Well, I don't see what I can do," said the skipper lazily. "What 'd you let 'em for?"

"You know what Bill is, sir," said Ned. "I'm an old man, cook's no good, and unless Simpson has a bit o' raw beef for his eyes, he won't be able to see for a week."

"Rubbish!" said the skipper jocularly. "Don't tell me, three men all afraid o' one ghost. I shan't interfere. Don't you know what to do?"

"No, sir," said Ned eagerly.

"Go up and read the Prayer-book to him, and he'll vanish in a cloud of smoke," said the skipper.

Ned gazed at him for a moment speechlessly, and then going up on deck leaned over the side and swore himself faint. The cook and Simpson came up and listened respectfully, contenting themselves with an occasional suggestion when the old man's memory momentarily failed him.

For the rest of the voyage the two culprits suffered all the inconvenience peculiar to a loss of citizenship. The skipper blandly ignored them, and on two or three occasions gave great offence by attempting to walk through Bill as he stood on the deck. Speculation was rife in the forecastle as to what would happen when they got ashore, and it was not until Northsea was sighted that the skipper showed his hand. Then he appeared on deck with their effects done up neatly in two bundles, and pitched them on the hatches. The crew stood and eyed him expectantly.

"Ned," said the skipper sharply.

"Sir," said the old man.

"As soon as we're made fast," said the other, "I want you to go ashore for me and fetch an undertaker and a policeman. I can't quite make up my mind which we want."

"Ay, ay, sir," murmured the old man.

The skipper turned away, and seizing the helm from the mate took his ship in. He was so intent upon this business that he appeared not to notice the movements of Bill and Tommy as they edged nervously towards their bundles, and waited impatiently for the schooner to get alongside the quay. Then he turned to the mate and burst into a loud laugh as the couple, bending suddenly, snatched up their bundles, and, clambering up the side ashore and took to their heels. The mate too, and a faint but mirthless echo came from the other end of the schooner.

THE CONSTABLE'S MOVE

Mr. Bob Grummit sat in the kitchen with his corduroy-clad legs stretched on the fender. His wife's half-eaten dinner was getting cold on the table; Mr. Grummit, who was badly in need of cheering up, emptied her half-empty glass of beer and wiped his lips with the back of his hand.

"Come away, I tell you," he called. "D'ye hear? Come away. You'll be locked up if you don't."

He gave a little laugh at the sarcasm, and sticking his short pipe in his mouth lurched slowly to the front-room door and scowled at his wife as she lurked at the back of the window watching intently the furniture which was being carried in next door.

"Come away or else you'll be locked up," repeated Mr. Grummit. "You mustn't look at policemen's furniture; it's agin the law."

Mrs. Grummit made no reply, but, throwing appearances to the winds, stepped to the window until her nose touched, as a walnut sideboard with bevelled glass back was tenderly borne inside under the personal supervision of Police-Constable Evans.

"They'll be 'aving a pianner next," said the indignant Mr. Grummit, peering from the depths of the room.

"They've got one," responded his wife; "there's the end if it stickin' up in the van."

Mr. Grummit advanced and regarded the end fixedly. "Did you throw all them tin cans and things into their yard wot I told you to?" he demanded.

"He picked up three of 'em while I was upstairs," replied his wife. "I 'eard 'im tell her that they'd come in handy for paint and things."

"That's 'ow coppers get on and buy pianners," said the incensed Mr. Grummit, "sneaking other people's property. I didn't tell you to throw good 'uns over, did I? Wot d'ye mean by it?"

Mrs. Grummit made no reply, but watched with bated breath the triumphal entrance of the piano. The carman set it tenderly on the narrow footpath, while P. C. Evans, stooping low, examined it at all points, and Mrs. Evans, raising the lid, struck a few careless chords.

"Showing off," explained Mrs. Grummit, with a half turn; "and she's got fingers like carrots."

"It's a disgrace to Mulberry Gardens to 'ave a copper come and live in it," said the indignant Grummit; "and to come and live next to me!— that's what I can't get over. To come and live next door to a man wot has been fined twice, and both times wrong. Why, for two pins I'd go in and smash 'is pianner first and 'im after it. He won't live 'ere long, you take my word for it."

"Why not?" inquired his wife.

"Why?" repeated Mr. Grummit. "Why? Why, becos I'll make the place too 'ot to hold him. Ain't there enough houses in Tunwich without 'im a-coming and living next door to me?"

For a whole week the brain concealed in Mr. Grummit's bullet-shaped head worked in vain, and his temper got correspondingly bad. The day after the Evans' arrival he had found his yard littered with tins which he recognized as old acquaintances, and since that time they had travelled backwards and forwards with monotonous regularity. They sometimes made as many as three journeys a day, and on one occasion the heavens opened to drop a battered tin bucket on the back of Mr. Grummit as he was tying his bootlace. Five minutes later he spoke of the outrage to Mr. Evans, who had come out to admire the sunset.

"I heard something fall," said the constable, eyeing the pail curiously.

"You threw it," said Mr. Grummit, breathing furiously.

"Me? Nonsense," said the other, easily. "I was having tea in the parlour with my wife and my mother-in-law, and my brother Joe and his young lady."

"Any more of 'em?" demanded the hapless Mr. Grummit, aghast at this list of witnesses for an alibi.

"It ain't a bad pail, if you look at it properly," said the constable. "I should keep it if I was you; unless the owner offers a reward for it. It'll hold enough water for your wants."

Mr. Grummit flung indoors and, after wasting some time concocting impossible measures of retaliation with his sympathetic partner, went off to discuss affairs with his intimates at the Bricklayers' Arms. The company, although unanimously agreeing that Mr. Evans ought to be boiled, were miserably deficient in ideas as to the means by which such a desirable end was to be attained.

"Make 'im a laughing-stock, that's the best thing," said an elderly labourer. "The police don't like being laughed at."

"'Ow?" demanded Mr. Grummit, with some asperity.

"There's plenty o' ways," said the old man.

"I should find 'em out fast enough if I 'ad a bucket dropped on my back, I know."

Mr. Grummit made a retort the feebleness of which was somewhat balanced by its ferocity, and subsided into glum silence. His back still ached, but, despite that aid to intellectual effort, the only ways he could imagine of making the constable look foolish contained an almost certain risk of hard labour for himself.

He pondered the question for a week, and meanwhile the tins—to the secret disappointment of Mr. Evans—remained untouched in his yard. For the whole of the time he went about looking, as Mrs. Grummit expressed it, as though his dinner had disagreed with him.

"I've been talking to old Bill Smith," he said, suddenly, as he came in one night.

Mrs. Grummit looked up, and noticed with wifely pleasure that he was looking almost cheerful.

"He's given me a tip," said Mr. Grummit, with a faint smile; "a copper mustn't come into a free-born Englishman's 'ouse unless he's invited."

"Wot of it?" inquired his wife. "You wasn't think of asking him in, was you?"

Mr. Grummit regarded her almost play-fully. "If a copper comes in without being told to," he continued, "he gets into trouble for it. Now d'ye see?"

"But he won't come," said the puzzled Mrs. Grummit.

Mr. Grummit winked. "Yes 'e will if you scream loud enough," he retorted. "Where's the copper-stick?"

"Have you gone mad?" demanded his wife, "or do you think I 'ave?"

"You go up into the bedroom," said Mr. Grummit, emphasizing his remarks with his forefinger. "I come up and beat the bed black and blue with the copper-stick; you scream for mercy and call out 'Help!' 'Murder!' and things like that. Don't call out 'Police!' cos Bill ain't sure about that part. Evans comes bursting in to save your life—I'll leave the door on the latch—and there you are. He's sure to get into trouble for it. Bill said so. He's made a study o' that sort o' thing."

Mrs. Grummit pondered this simple plan so long that her husband began to lose patience. At last, against her better sense, she rose and fetched the weapon in question.

"And you be careful what you're hitting," she said, as they went upstairs to bed. "We'd better have 'igh words first, I s'pose?"

"You pitch into me with your tongue," said Mr. Grummit, amiably.

Mrs. Grummit, first listening to make sure that the constable and his wife were in the bedroom the other side of the flimsy wall, complied, and in a voice that rose gradually to a piercing falsetto told Mr. Grummit things that had been rankling in her mind for some months. She raked up misdemeanours that he had long since forgotten, and, not content with that, had a fling at the entire Grummit family, beginning with her mother-in-law and ending with Mr. Grummit's youngest sister. The hand that held the copper-stick itched.

"Any more to say?" demanded Mr. Grummit advancing upon her.

Mrs. Grummit emitted a genuine shriek, and Mr. Grummit, suddenly remembering himself, stopped short and attacked the bed with extraordinary fury. The room resounded with the blows, and the efforts of Mrs. Grummit were a revelation even to her husband.

"I can hear 'im moving," whispered Mr. Grummit, pausing to take breath.

"Mur—der!" wailed his wife. "Help! Help!"

Mr. Grummit, changing the stick into his left hand, renewed the attack; Mrs. Grummit, whose voice was becoming exhausted, sought a temporary relief in moans.

"Is—he—deaf?" panted the wife-beater, "or wot?"

He knocked over a chair, and Mrs. Grummit contrived another frenzied scream. A loud knocking sounded on the wall.

"Hel—lp!" moaned Mrs. Grummit.

"Halloa, there!" came the voice of the constable. "Why don't you keep that baby quiet? We can't get a wink of sleep."

Mr. Grummit dropped the stick on the bed and turned a dazed face to his wife.

"He—he's afraid—to come in," he gasped. "Keep it up, old gal."

He took up the stick again and Mrs. Grummit did her best, but the heart had gone out of the thing, and he was about to give up the task as hopeless when the door below was heard to open with a bang.

"Here he is," cried the jubilant Grummit. "Now!"

His wife responded, and at the same moment the bedroom door was flung open, and her brother, who had been hastily fetched by the neighbours on the other side, burst into the room and with one hearty blow sent Mr. Grummit sprawling.

"Hit my sister, will you?" he roared, as the astounded Mr. Grummit rose. "Take that!"

Mr. Grummit took it, and several other favours, while his wife, tugging at her brother, endeavoured to explain. It was not, however, until Mr. Grummit claimed the usual sanctuary of the defeated by refusing to rise that she could make herself heard.

"Joke?" repeated her brother, incredulously. "Joke?"

Mrs. Grummit in a husky voice explained.

Her brother passed from incredulity to amazement and from amazement to mirth. He sat down gurgling, and the indignant face of the injured Grummit only added to his distress.

"Best joke I ever heard in my life," he said, wiping his eyes. "Don't look at me like that, Bob; I can't bear it."

"Get off 'ome," responded Mr. Grummit, glowering at him.

"There's a crowd outside, and half the doors in the place open," said the other. "Well, it's a good job there's no harm done. So long."

He passed, beaming, down the stairs, and Mr. Grummit, drawing near the window, heard him explaining in a broken voice to the neighbours outside. Strong men patted him on the back and urged him gruffly to say what he had to say and laugh afterwards. Mr. Grummit turned from the window, and in a slow and stately fashion prepared to retire for the night. Even the sudden and startling disappearance of Mrs. Grummit as she got into bed failed to move him.

"The bed's broke, Bob," she said faintly.

"Beds won't last forever," he said, shortly; "sleep on the floor."

Mrs. Grummit clambered out, and after some trouble secured the bedclothes and made up a bed in a corner of the room. In a short time she was fast asleep; but her husband, broad awake, spent the night in devising further impracticable schemes for the discomfiture of the foe next door.

He saw Mr. Evans next morning as he passed on his way to work. The constable was at the door smoking in his shirt-sleeves, and Mr. Grummit felt instinctively that he was waiting there to see him pass.

"I heard you last night," said the constable, playfully. "My word! Good gracious!"

"Wot's the matter with you?" demanded Mr. Grummit, stopping short.

The constable stared at him. "She has been knocking you about," he gasped. "Why, it must ha' been you screaming, then! I thought it sounded loud. Why don't you go and get a summons and have her locked up? I should be pleased to take her."

Mr. Grummit faced him, quivering with passion. "Wot would it cost if I set about you?" he demanded, huskily.

"Two months," said Mr. Evans, smiling serenely; "p'r'aps three."

Mr. Grummit hesitated and his fists clenched nervously. The constable, lounging against his door-post, surveyed him with a dispassionate smile. "That would be besides what you'd get from me," he said, softly.

"Come out in the road," said Mr. Grummit, with sudden violence.

"It's agin the rules," said Mr. Evans; "sorry I can't. Why not go and ask your wife's brother to oblige you?"

He went in laughing and closed the door, and Mr. Grummit, after a frenzied outburst, proceeded on his way, returning the smiles of such acquaintances as he passed with an icy stare or a strongly-worded offer to make them laugh the other side of their face. The rest of the day he spent in working so hard that he had no time to reply to the anxious inquiries of his fellow-workmen.

He came home at night glum and silent, the hardship of not being able to give Mr. Evans his deserts without incurring hard labour having weighed on his spirits all day. To avoid the annoyance of the piano next door, which was slowly and reluctantly yielding up "*The Last Rose of Summer*" note by note, he went out at the back, and the first thing he saw was Mr. Evans mending his path with tins and other bric-a-brac.

"Nothing like it," said the constable, looking up. "Your missus gave 'em to us this morning. A little gravel on top, and there you are."

He turned whistling to his work again, and the other, after endeavouring in vain to frame a suitable reply, took a seat on an inverted wash-tub and lit his pipe. His one hope was that Constable Evans was going to try and cultivate a garden.

The hope was realized a few days later, and Mr. Grummit at the back window sat gloating over a dozen fine geraniums, some lobelias and calceolarias, which decorated the constable's plot of ground. He could not sleep for thinking of them.

He rose early the next morning, and, after remarking to Mrs. Grummit that Mr. Evans's flowers looked as though they wanted rain, went off to his work. The cloud which had been on his spirits for some time had lifted, and he whistled as he walked. The sight of flowers in front windows added to his good humour.

He was still in good spirits when he left off work that afternoon, but some slight hesitation about returning home sent him to the Brick-layers' firms instead. He stayed there until closing time, and then, being still disinclined for home, paid a visit to Bill Smith, who lived the other side of Tunwich. By the time he started for home it was nearly midnight.

The outskirts of the town were deserted and the houses in darkness. The clock of Tunwich church struck twelve, and the last stroke was just dying away as he turned a corner and ran almost into the arms of the man he had been trying to avoid.

"Halloa!" said Constable Evans, sharply. "Here, I want a word with you."

Mr. Grummit quailed. "With me, sir?" he said, with involuntary respect.

"What have you been doing to my flowers?" demanded the other, hotly.

"Flowers?" repeated Mr. Grummit, as though the word were new to him. "Flowers? What flowers?"

"You know well enough," retorted the constable. "You got over my fence last night and smashed all my flowers down."

"You be careful wot you're saying," urged Mr. Grummit. "Why, I love flowers. You don't mean to tell me that all them beautiful flowers wot you put in so careful 'as been spoiled?"

"You know all about it," said the constable, choking. "I shall take out a summons against you for it."

"Ho!" said Mr. Grummit. "And wot time do you say it was when I done it?"

"Never you mind the time," said the other.

"Cos it's important," said Mr. Grummit.

"My wife's brother—the one you're so fond of—slept in my 'ouse last night. He was ill arf the night, pore chap; but, come to think of it, it'll make 'im a good witness for my innocence."

"If I wasn't a policeman," said Mr. Evans, speaking with great deliberation, "I'd take hold o' you, Bob Grummit, and I'd give you the biggest hiding you've ever had in your life."

"If you wasn't a policeman," said Mr. Grummit, yearningly, "I'd arf murder you."

The two men eyed each other wistfully, loth to part.

"If I gave you what you deserve I should get into trouble," said the constable.

"If I gave you a quarter of wot you ought to 'ave I should go to quod," sighed Mr. Grummit.

"I wouldn't put you there," said the constable, earnestly; "I swear I wouldn't."

"Everything's beautiful and quiet," said Mr. Grummit, trembling with eagerness, "and I wouldn't say a word to a soul. I'll take my solemn davit I wouldn't."

"When I think o' my garden—" began the constable. With a sudden movement he knocked off Mr. Grummit's cap, and then, seizing him by the coat, began to hustle him along the road. In the twinkling of an eye they had closed.

Tunwich church chimed the half-hour as they finished, and Mr. Grummit, forgetting his own injuries, stood smiling at the wreck before him. The constable's helmet had been smashed and trodden on; his uniform was torn and covered with blood and dirt, and his good looks marred for a fortnight at least. He stooped with a groan, and, recovering his helmet, tried mechanically to punch it into shape. He stuck the battered relic on his head, and Mr. Grummit fell back—awed, despite himself.

"It was a fair fight," he stammered.

The constable waved him away. "Get out o' my sight before I change my mind," he said, fiercely; "and mind, if you say a word about this it'll be the worse for you."

"Do you think I've gone mad?" said the other. He took another look at his victim and, turning away, danced fantastically along the road home. The constable, making his way to a gas-lamp, began to inspect damages.

They were worse even than he had thought, and, leaning against the lamp-post, he sought in vain for an explanation that, in the absence of a prisoner, would satisfy the inspector. A button which was hanging by a thread fell tinkling on to the footpath, and he had just picked it up and placed it in his pocket when a faint distant outcry broke upon his ear.

He turned and walked as rapidly as his condition would permit in the direction of the noise. It became louder and more imperative, and cries of "Police!" became distinctly audible. He quickened into a run, and turning a corner beheld a little knot of people standing at the gate of a large house. Other people only partially clad were hastening to-wards them. The constable arrived out of breath.

"Better late than never," said the owner of the house, sarcastically.

Mr. Evans, breathing painfully, supported himself with his hand on the fence.

"They went that way, but I suppose you didn't see them," continued the householder. "Halloa!" he added, as somebody opened the hall door and the constable's damaged condition became visible in the gas-light. "Are you hurt?"

"Yes," said Mr. Evans, who was trying hard to think clearly. To gain time he blew a loud call on his whistle.

"The rascals!" continued the other. "I think I should know the big chap with a beard again, but the others were too quick for me."

Mr. Evans blew his whistle again—thoughtfully. The opportunity seemed too good to lose.

"Did they get anything?" he inquired.

"Not a thing," said the owner, triumphantly. "I was disturbed just in time."

The constable gave a slight gulp. "I saw the three running by the side of the road," he said, slowly. "Their behaviour seemed suspicious, so I collared the big one, but they set on me like wild cats. They had me down three times; the last time I laid my head open against the kerb, and when I came to my senses again they had gone."

He took off his battered helmet with a flourish and, amid a murmur of sympathy, displayed a nasty cut on his head. A sergeant and a constable, both running, appeared round the corner and made towards' them.

"Get back to the station and make your report," said the former, as Constable Evans, in a somewhat defiant voice, repeated his story. "You've done your best; I can see that."

Mr. Evans, enacting to perfection the part of a wounded hero, limped painfully off, praying devoutly as he went that the criminals might make good their escape. If not, he reflected that the word of a policeman was at least equal to that of three burglars.

He repeated his story at the station, and, after having his head dressed, was sent home and advised to keep himself quiet for a day or two. He was off duty for four days, and, the Tunwich Gazette having devoted a column to the affair, headed "A Gallant Constable," modestly secluded himself from the public gaze for the whole of that time.

To Mr. Grummit, who had read the article in question until he could have repeated it backwards, this modesty was particularly trying. The constable's yard was deserted and the front door ever closed. Once Mr. Grummit even went so far as to tap with his nails on the front parlour window, and the only response was the sudden lowering of the blind. It was not until a week afterwards that his eyes were gladdened by a sight of the constable sitting in his yard; and fearing that even then he might escape him, he ran out on tip-toe and put his face over the fence before the latter was aware of his presence.

"Wot about that 'ere burglary?" he demanded in truculent tones.

"Good evening, Grummit," said the constable, with a patronizing air.

"Wot about that burglary?" repeated Mr. Grummit, with a scowl. "I don't believe you ever saw a burglar."

Mr. Evans rose and stretched himself gracefully. "You'd better run indoors, my good man," he said, slowly.

"Telling all them lies about burglars," continued the indignant Mr. Grummit, producing his newspaper and waving it. "Why, I gave you that black eye, I smashed your 'elmet, I cut your silly 'ead open, I—"

"You've been drinking," said the other, severely.

"You mean to say I didn't?" demanded Mr. Grummit, ferociously.

Mr. Evans came closer and eyed him steadily. "I don't know what you're talking about," he said, calmly.

Mr. Grummit, about to speak, stopped appalled at such hardihood.

"Of course, if you mean to say that you were one o' them burglars," continued the constable, "why, say it and I'll take you with pleasure. Come to think of it, I did seem to remember one o' their voices."

Mr. Grummit, with his eyes fixed on the other's, backed a couple of yards and breathed heavily.

"About your height, too, he was," mused the constable. "I hope for your sake you haven't been saying to anybody else what you said to me just now."

Mr. Grummit shook his head. "Not a word," he faltered.

"That's all right, then," said Mr. Evans. "I shouldn't like to be hard on a neighbour; not that we shall be neighbours much longer."

Mr. Grummit, feeling that a reply was expected of him, gave utterance to a feeble "Oh!"

"No," said Mr. Evans, looking round disparagingly. "It ain't good enough for us now; I was promoted to sergeant this morning. A sergeant can't live in a common place like this."

Mr. Grummit, a prey to a sickening fear, drew near the fence again. "A— a sergeant?" he stammered.

Mr. Evans smiled and gazed carefully at a distant cloud. "For my bravery with them burglars the other night, Grummit," he said, modestly. "I might have waited years if it hadn't been for them."

He nodded to the frantic Grummit and turned away; Mr. Grummit, without any adieu at all, turned and crept back to the house.

CONTRABAND OF WAR

A small but strong lamp was burning in the fo'c'sle of the schooner Greyhound, by the light of which a middle-aged seaman of sedate appearance sat crocheting an antimacassar. Two other men were snoring with deep content in their bunks, while a small, bright-eyed boy sat up in his, reading adventurous fiction.

"Here comes old Dan," said the man with the anti-macassar warningly, as a pair of sea boots appeared at the top of the companion-ladder; "better not let him see you with that paper, Billee."

The boy thrust it beneath his blankets, and, lying down, closed his eyes as the new comer stepped on to the floor.

"All asleep?" inquired the latter.

The other man nodded, and Dan, without any further parley, crossed over to the sleepers and shook them roughly.

"Eh! wha's matter?" inquired the sleepers plaintively.

"Git up," said Dan impressively, "I want to speak to you. Something important."

With sundry growls the men complied, and, thrusting their legs out of their bunks, rolled on to the locker, and sat crossly waiting for information.

"I want to do a pore chap a good turn," said Dan, watching them narrowly out of his little black eyes, "an' I want you to help me; an' the boy too. It's never too young to do good to your fellow-creatures, Billy."

"I know it ain't," said Billy, taking this as permission to join the group; "I helped a drunken man home once when I was only ten years old, an' when I was only—"

The speaker stopped, not because he had come to the end of his remarks, but because one of the seamen had passed his arm around his neck and was choking him.

"Go on," said the man calmly; "I've got him. Spit it out, Dan, and none of your sermonising."

"Well, it's like this, Joe," said the old man; "here's a pore chap, a young sojer from the depot here, an' he's cut an' run. He's been in hiding in a cottage up the road two days, and he wants to git to London, and git honest work and employment, not shooting, an' stabbing, an' bayoneting—"

"Stow it," said Joe impatiently.

"He daren't go to the railway station, and he dursen't go outside in his uniform," continued Dan. "My 'art bled for the pore young feller, an' I've promised to give 'im a little trip to London with us. The people he's staying with won't have him no longer. They've only got one bed, and directly he sees any sojers coming he goes an' gits into it, whether he's got his boots on or not."

"Have you told the skipper?" inquired Joe sardonically.

"I won't deceive you, Joe, I 'ave not," replied the old man. "He'll have to stay down here of a daytime, an' only come on deck of a night when it's our watch. I told 'im what a lot of good-'arted chaps you was, and how—"

"How much is he going to give you?" inquired Joe impatiently.

"It's only fit and proper he should pay a little for the passage," said Dan.

"How MUCH?" demanded Joe, banging the little triangular table with his fist, and thereby causing the man with the antimacassar to drop a couple of stitches.

"Twenty-five shillings," said old Dan reluctantly; "an' I'll spend the odd five shillings on you chaps when we git to Limehouse."

"I don't want your money," said Joe; "there's a empty bunk he can have; and mind, you take all the responsibility—I won't have nothing to do with it."

"Thanks, Joe," said the old man, with a sigh of relief; "he's a nice young chap, you're sure to take to him. I'll go and give him the tip to come aboard at once."

He ran up on deck again and whistled softly, and a figure, which had been hiding behind a pile of empties, came out, and, after looking cautiously around, dropped noiselessly on to the schooner's deck, and followed its protector below.

"Good evening, mates," said the linesman, gazing curiously and anxiously round him as he deposited a bundle on the table, and laid his swagger cane beside it.

"What's your height?" inquired Joe abruptly. "Seven foot?"

"No, only six foot four," said the new arrival, modestly. "I'm not proud of it. It's much easier for a small man to slip off than a big one."

"It licks me," said Joe thoughtfully, "what they want 'em back for—I should think they'd be glad to git rid o' such"—he paused a moment while politeness struggled with feeling, and added, "skunks."

"P'raps I've a reason for being a skunk, p'raps I haven't," retorted Private Smith, as his face fell.

"This'll be your bunk," interposed Dan hastily; "put your things in there, and when you are in yourself you'll be as comfortable as a oyster in its shell."

The visitor complied, and, first extracting from the bundle some tins of meat and a bottle of whiskey, which he placed upon the table, nervously requested the honour of the present company to supper. With the exception of Joe, who churlishly climbed back into his bunk, the men complied, all agreeing that boys of Billy's age should be reared on strong teetotal principles.

Supper over, Private Smith and his protectors retired to their couches, where the former lay in much anxiety until two in the morning, when they got under way.

"It's all right, my lad," said Dan, after the watch had been set, as he came and stood by the deserter's bunk; "I 've saved you—I've saved you for twenty-five shillings."

"I wish it was more," said Private Smith politely.

The old man sighed—and waited.

"I'm quite cleaned out, though," continued the deserter, "except fi'pence ha'penny. I shall have to risk going home in my uniform as it is."

"Ah, you'll get there all right," said Dan cheerfully; "and when you get home no doubt you 've got friends, and if it seems to you as you 'd like to give a little more to them as assisted you in the hour of need, you won't be ungrateful, my lad, I know. You ain't the sort."

With these words old Dan, patting him affectionately, retired, and the soldier lay trying to sleep in his narrow quarters until he was aroused by a grip on his arm.

"If you want a mouthful of fresh air you 'd better come on deck now," said the voice of Joe; "it's my watch. You can get all the sleep you want in the daytime."

Glad to escape from such stuffy quarters, Private Smith clambered out of his bunk and followed the other on deck. It was a fine clear night, and the schooner was going along under a light breeze; the seaman took the wheel, and, turning to his companion, abruptly inquired what he meant by deserting and worrying them with six foot four of underdone lobster.

"It's all through my girl," said Private Smith meekly; "first she jilted me, and made me join the army; now she's chucked the other fellow, and wrote to me to go back."

"An' now I s'pose the other chap'll take your place in the army," said Joe. "Why, a gal like that could fill a regiment, if she liked. Pah! They'll nab you too, in that uniform, and you'll get six months, and have to finish your time as well."

"It's more than likely," said the soldier gloomily. "I've got to tramp to Manchester in these clothes, as far as I can see."

"What did you give old Dan all your money for?" inquired Joe.

"I was only thinking of getting away at first," said Smith, "and I had to take what was offered."

"Well, I'll do what I can for you," said the seaman. "If you're in love, you ain't responsible for your actions. I remember the first time I got the chuck. I went into a public-house bar, and smashed all the glass and bottles I could get at. I felt as though I must do something. If you were only shorter, I'd lend you some clothes."

"You're a brick," said the soldier gratefully.

"I haven't got any money I could lend you either," said Joe. "I never do have any, somehow. But clothes you must have."

He fell into deep thought, and cocked his eye aloft as though contemplating a cutting-out expedition on the sails, while the soldier, sitting on the side of the ship, waited hopefully for a miracle.

"You'd better get below again," said Joe presently.

"There seems to be somebody moving below; and if the skipper sees you, you're done. He's a regular Tartar, and he's got a brother what's a sergeant-major in the army. He'd give you up d'rectly if he spotted you."

"I'm off," said Smith; and with long, cat-like strides he disappeared swiftly below.

For two days all went well, and Dan was beginning to congratulate himself upon his little venture, when his peace of mind was rudely disturbed. The crew were down below, having their tea, when Billy, who had been to the galley for hot water, came down, white and scared.

"Look here," he said nervously, "I've not had anything to do with this chap being aboard, have I?"

"What's the matter?" inquired Dan quickly.

"It's all found out," said Billy.

"WHAT!" cried the crew simultaneously.

"Leastways, it will be," said the youth, correcting himself. "You'd better chuck him overboard while you've got time. I heard the cap'n tell the mate as he was coming down in the fo'c'sle to-morrow morning to look round. He's going to have it painted."

"This," said Dan, in the midst of a painful pause, "this is what comes of helping a fellow-creature. What's to be done?"

"Tell the skipper the fo'c'sle don't want painting," suggested Billy.

The agonised old seaman, carefully putting down his saucer of tea, cuffed his head spitefully.

"It's a smooth sea," said he, looking at the perturbed countenance of Private Smith, "'an there's a lot of shipping about. If I was a deserter, sooner than be caught, I would slip overboard to-night with a lifebelt and take my chance."

"I wouldn't," said Mr. Smith, with much decision.

"You wouldn't? Not if you was quite near another ship?" cooed Dan.

"Not if I was near fifty blooming ships, all trying to see which could pick me up first," replied Mr. Smith, with some heat.

"Then we shall have to leave you to your fate," said Dan solemnly. "If a man's unreasonable, his best friends can do nothing for him."

"Chuck all his clothes overboard, anyway," said Billy.

"That's a good idea o' the boy's. You leave his ears alone," said Joe, stopping the ready hand of the exasperated Dan. "He's got more sense than any of us. Can you think of anything else, Billy? What shall we do then?"

The eyes of all were turned upon their youthful deliverer, those of Mr. Smith being painfully prominent. It was a proud moment for Billy, and he sat silent for some time, with a look of ineffable wisdom and thought upon his face. At length he spoke.

"Let somebody else have a turn," he said generously.

The voice of the antimacassar worker broke the silence.

"Paint him all over with stripes of different-coloured paint, and let him pretend he's mad, and didn't know how he got here," he said, with an uncontrollable ring of pride at the idea, which was very coldly received, Private Smith being noticeably hard on it.

"I know," said Billy shrilly, clapping his hands. "I've got it, I've got it. After he's chucked his clothes overboard to-night, let him go overboard too, with a line."

"And tow him the rest o' the way, and chuck biscuits to him, I suppose," snarled Dan.

"No," said the youthful genius scornfully; "pretend he's been upset from a boat, and has been swimming about, and we heard him cry out for help and rescued him."

"It's about the best way out of it," said Joe, after some deliberation; "it's warm weather, and you won't take no harm, mate. Do it in my watch, and I'll pull you out directly."

"Wouldn't it do if you just chucked a bucket of water over me and SAID you'd pulled me out," suggested the victim. "The other thing seems a downright LIE."

"No," said Billy authoritatively, "you've got to look half-drowned, and swallow a lot of water, and your eyes be all bloodshot."

Everybody being eager for the adventure, except Private Smith, the arrangements were at once concluded, and the approach of night impatiently awaited. It was just before midnight when Smith, who had forgotten for the time his troubles in sleep, was shaken into wakefulness.

"Cold water, sir?" said Billy gleefully.

In no mood for frivolity, Private Smith rose and followed the youth on deck. The air struck him as chill as he stood there; but, for all that, it was with a sense of relief that he saw Her Majesty's uniform go over the side and sink into the dark water.

"He don't look much with his padding off, does he?" said Billy, who had been eyeing him critically.

"You go below," said Dan sharply.

"Garn," said Billy indignantly; "I want to see the fun as well as you do. I thought of it."

"Fun?" said the old man severely. "Fun? To see a feller creature suffering, and perhaps drowned—"

"I don't think I had better go," said the victim; "it seems rather underhand."

"Yes, you will," said Joe. "Wind this line round an' round your arm, and just swim about gently till I pull you in."

Sorely against his inclination Private Smith took hold of the line, and, hanging over the side of the schooner, felt the temperature with his foot, and, slowly and tenderly, with many little gasps, committed his body to the deep. Joe paid out the line and waited, letting out more line, when the man in the water, who was getting anxious, started to come in hand over hand.

"That'll do," said Dan at length.

"I think it will," said Joe, and, putting his hand to his mouth, gave a mighty shout. It was answered almost directly by startled roars from the cabin, and the skipper and mate came rushing hastily upon deck, to see the crew, in their sleeping gear, forming an excited group round Joe, and peering eagerly over the side.

"What's the matter?" demanded the skipper.

"Somebody in the water, sir," said Joe, relinquishing the wheel to one of the other seamen, and hauling in the line. "I heard a cry from the water and threw a line, and, by gum, I've hooked it!"

He hauled in, lustily aided by the skipper, until the long white body of Private Smith, blanched with the cold, came bumping against the schooner's side.

"It's a mermaid," said the mate, who was inclined to be superstitious, as he peered doubtfully down at it. "Let it go, Joe."

"Haul it in, boys," said the skipper impatiently; and two of the men clambered over the side and, stooping down, raised it from the water.

In the midst of a puddle, which he brought with him, Private Smith was laid on the deck, and, waving his arms about, fought wildly for his breath.

"Fetch one of them empties," said the skipper quickly, as he pointed to some barrels ranged along the side.

The men rolled one over, and then aided the skipper in placing the long fair form of their visitor across it, and to trundle it lustily up and down the deck, his legs forming convenient handles for the energetic operators.

"He's coming round," said the mate, checking them; "he's speaking. How do you feel, my poor fellow?"

He put his ear down, but the action was unnecessary. Private Smith felt bad, and, in the plainest English he could think of at the moment, said so distinctly.

"He's swearing," said the mate. "He ought to be ashamed of himself."

"Yes," said the skipper austerely; "and him so near death too. How did you get in the water?"

"Went for a—swim," panted Smith surlily.

"SWIM?" echoed the skipper. "Why, we're ten miles from land!"

"His mind's wandering, pore feller," interrupted Joe hurriedly. "What boat did you fall out of, matey?"

"A row-boat," said Smith, trying to roll out of reach of the skipper, who was down on his knees flaying him alive with a roller-towel. "I had to undress in the water to keep afloat. I've lost all my clothes."

"Pore feller," said Dan.

"A gold watch and chain, my purse, and three of the nicest fellers that ever breathed," continued Smith, who was now entering into the spirit of the thing.

"Poor chaps," said the skipper solemnly. "Any of 'em leave any family?"

"Four," said Smith sadly.

"Children?" queried the mate.

"Families," said Smith.

"Look here," said the mate, but the watchful Joe interrupted him.

"His mind's wandering," said he hastily. "He can't count, pore chap. We'd better git him to bed."

"Ah, do," said the skipper, and, assisted by his friends, the rescued man was half led, half carried below and put between the blankets, where he lay luxuriously sipping a glass of brandy and water, sent from the cabin.

"How'd I do it?" he inquired, with a satisfied air.

"There was no need to tell all them lies about it," said Dan sharply; "instead of one little lie you told half-a-dozen. I don't want nothing more to do with you. You start afresh now, like a new-born babe."

"All right," said Smith shortly; and, being very much fatigued with his exertions, and much refreshed by the brandy, fell into a deep and peaceful sleep.

The morning was well advanced when he awoke, and the fo'c'sle empty except for the faithful Joe, who was standing by his side, with a heap of clothing under his arm.

"Try these on," said he, as Smith stared at him half awake; "they'll be better than nothing, at any rate."

The soldier leaped from his bunk and gratefully proceeded to dress himself, Joe eyeing him critically as the trousers climbed up his long legs, and the sleeves of the jacket did their best to conceal his elbows.

"What do I look like?" he inquired anxiously, as he finished.

"Six foot an' a half o' misery," piped the shrill voice of Billy promptly, as he thrust his head in at the fo'c'sle. "You can't go to church in those clothes."

"Well, they'll do for the ship, but you can't go ashore in 'em," said Joe, as he edged towards the ladder, and suddenly sprang up a step or two to let fly at the boy, "The old man wants to see you; be careful what you say to him."

With a very unsuccessful attempt to appear unconscious of the figure he cut, Smith went up on deck for the interview.

"We can't do anything until we get to London," said the skipper, as he made copious notes of Smith's adventures. "As soon as we get there, I'll lend you the money to telegraph to your friends to tell 'em you're safe and to send you some clothes, and of course you'll have free board and lodging till it comes, and I'll write out an account of it for the newspapers."

"You're very good," said Smith blankly.

"And I don't know what you are," said the skipper, interrogatively; "but you ought to go in for swimming as a profession—six hours' swimming about like that is wonderful."

"You don't know what you can do till you have to," said Smith modestly, as he backed slowly away; "but I never want to see the water again as long as I live."

The two remaining days of their passage passed all too quickly for the men, who were casting about for some way out of the difficulty which they foresaw would arise when they reached London.

"If you'd only got decent clothes," said Joe, as they passed Gravesend, "you could go off and send a telegram, and not come back; but you couldn't go five yards in them things without having a crowd after you."

"I shall have to be taken I s'pose," said Smith moodily.

"An' poor old Dan'll get six months hard for helping you off," said Joe sympathetically, as a bright idea occurred to him.

"Rubbish!" said Dan uneasily. "He can stick to his tale of being upset; anyway, the skipper saw him pulled out of the water. He's too honest a chap to get an old man into trouble for trying to help him."

"He must have a new rig out, Dan," said Joe softly. "You an' me'll go an' buy 'em. I'll do the choosing, and you'll do the paying. Why, it'll be a reg'lar treat for you to lay out a little money, Dan. We'll have quite an evening's shopping, everything of the best."

The infuriated Dan gasped for breath, and looked helplessly at the grinning crew.

"I'll see him—overboard first," he said furiously.

"Please yourself," said Joe shortly, "If he's caught you'll get six months. As it is, you've got a chance of doing a nice, kind little Christian act, becos, o' course, that twenty-five bob you got out of him won't anything like pay for his toggery."

Almost beside himself with indignation, the old man moved off, and said not another word until they were made fast to the wharf at Limehouse. He did not even break silence when Joe, taking him affectionately by the arm, led him aft to the skipper.

"Me an' Dan, sir," said Joe very respectfully, "would like to go ashore for a little shopping. Dan has very kindly offered to lend that pore chap the money for some clothes, and he wants me to go with him to help carry them."

"Ay, ay," said the skipper, with a benevolent smile at the aged philanthropist. "You'd better go at once, afore the shops shut."

"We'll run, sir," said Joe, and taking Dan by the arm, dragged him into the street at a trot.

Nearly a couple of hours passed before they returned, and no child watched with greater eagerness the opening of a birthday present than Smith watched the undoing of the numerous parcels with which they were laden.

"He's a reg'lar fairy godmother, ain't he?" said Joe, as Smith joyously dressed himself in a very presentable tweed suit, serviceable boots, and a bowler hat. "We had a dreadful job to get a suit big enough, an' the only one we could get was rather more money than we wanted to give, wasn't it, Dan?"

The fairy godmother strove manfully with his feelings.

"You'll do now," said Joe. "I ain't got much, but what I have you're welcome to." He put his hand into his pocket and pulled out some loose coin. "What have you got, mates?"

With decent good will the other men turned out their pockets, and, adding to the store, heartily pressed it upon the reluctant Smith, who, after shaking hands gratefully, followed Joe on deck.

"You've got enough to pay your fare," said the latter; "an' I've told the skipper you are going ashore to send off telegrams. If you send the money back to Dan, I'll never forgive you."

"I won't, then," said Smith firmly; "but I'll send theirs back to the other chaps. Good-bye."

Joe shook him by the hand again, and bade him go while the coast was clear, advice which Smith hastened to follow, though he turned and looked back to wave his hand to the crew, who had come up on deck silently to see him off; all but the philanthropist, who was down below with a stump of lead-pencil and a piece of paper doing sums.

THE CONVERT

Mr. Purnip took the arm of the new recruit and hung over him almost tenderly as they walked along; Mr. Billing, with a look of conscious virtue on his jolly face, listened with much satisfaction to his friend's compliments.

"It's such an example," said the latter. "Now we've got you the others will follow like sheep. You will be a bright lamp in the darkness."

"Wot's good enough for me ought to be good enough for them," said Mr. Billing, modestly. "They'd better not let me catch—"

"H'sh! H'sh!" breathed Mr. Purnip, tilting his hat and wiping his bald, benevolent head.

"I forgot," said the other, with something like a sigh. "No more fighting; but suppose somebody hits me?"

"Turn the other cheek," replied Mr. Purnip.

"They won't hit that; and when they see you standing there smiling at them—"

"After being hit?" interrupted Mr. Billing.

"After being hit," assented the other, "they'll be ashamed of themselves, and it'll hurt them more than if you struck them."

"Let's 'ope so," said the convert; "but it don't sound reasonable. I can hit a man pretty 'ard. Not that I'm bad-tempered, mind you; a bit quick, p'r'aps. And, after all, a good smack in the jaw saves any amount of argufying."

Mr. Purnip smiled, and, as they walked along, painted a glowing picture of the influence to be wielded by a first-class fighting-man who refused to fight. It was a rough neighbourhood, and he recognized with sorrow that more respect was paid to a heavy fist than to a noble intellect or a loving heart.

"And you combine them all," he said, patting his companion's arm.

Mr. Billing smiled. "You ought to know best," he said, modestly.

"You'll be surprised to find how easy it is," continued Mr. Purnip. "You will go from strength to strength. Old habits will disappear, and you will hardly know you have lost them. In a few months' time you will probably be wondering what you could ever have seen in beer, for example."

"I thought you said you didn't want me to give up beer?" said the other.

"We don't," said Mr. Purnip. "I mean that as you grow in stature you will simply lose the taste for it."

Mr. Billing came to a sudden full stop. "D'ye mean I shall lose my liking for a drop o' beer without being able to help myself?" he demanded, in an anxious voice.

"Of course, it doesn't happen in every case," he said, hastily.

Mr. Billing's features relaxed. "Well, let's 'ope I shall be one of the fortunate ones," he said, simply. "I can put up with a good deal, but when it comes to beer—"

"We shall see," said the other, smiling.

"We don't want to interfere with anybody's comfort; we want to make them happier, that's all. A little more kindness between man and man; a little more consideration for each other; a little more brightness in dull lives."

He paused at the corner of the street, and, with a hearty handshake, went off. Mr. Billing, a prey to somewhat mixed emotions, continued on his way home. The little knot of earnest men and women who had settled in the district to spread light and culture had been angling for him for some time. He wondered, as he walked, what particular bait it was that had done the mischief.

"They've got me at last," he remarked, as he opened the house-door and walked into his small kitchen. "I couldn't say 'no' to Mr. Purnip."

"Wish 'em joy," said Mrs. Billing, briefly. "Did you wipe your boots?"

Her husband turned without a word, and, retreating to the mat, executed a prolonged double-shuffle.

"You needn't wear it out," said the surprised Mrs. Billing.

"We've got to make people 'appier," said her husband, seriously; "be kinder to 'em, and brighten up their dull lives a bit. That's wot Mr. Purnip says."

"You'll brighten 'em up all right," declared Mrs. Billing, with a sniff. "I sha'n't forget last Tuesday week—no, not if I live to be a hundred. You'd ha' brightened up the police-station if I 'adn't got you home just in the nick of time."

Her husband, who was by this time busy under the scullery-tap, made no reply. He came from it spluttering, and, seizing a small towel, stood in the door-way burnishing his face and regarding his wife with a smile which Mr. Purnip himself could not have surpassed. He sat down to supper, and between bites explained in some detail the lines on which his future life was to be run. As an earnest of good faith, he consented, after a short struggle, to a slip of oil-cloth for the passage; a pair of vases for the front room; and a new and somewhat expensive corn-cure for Mrs. Billing.

"And let's 'ope you go on as you've begun," said that gratified lady. "There's something in old Purnip after all. I've been worrying you for months for that oilcloth. Are you going to help me wash up? Mr. Purnip would."

Mr. Billing appeared not to hear, and, taking up his cap, strolled slowly in the direction of the Blue Lion. It was a beautiful summer evening, and his bosom swelled as he thought of the improvements that a little brotherliness might effect in Elk Street. Engrossed in such ideas, it almost hurt him to find that, as he entered one door of the Blue Lion, two gentlemen, forgetting all about their beer, disappeared through the other.

"Wot 'ave they run away like that for?" he demanded, looking round. "I wouldn't hurt 'em."

"Depends on wot you call hurting, Joe," said a friend.

Mr. Billing shook his head. "They've no call to be afraid of me," he said, gravely. "I wouldn't hurt a fly; I've got a new 'art."

"A new wot?" inquired his friend, staring.

"A new 'art," repeated the other. "I've given up fighting and swearing, and drinking too much. I'm going to lead a new life and do all the good I can; I'm going—"

"Glory! Glory!" ejaculated a long, thin youth, and, making a dash for the door, disappeared.

"He'll know me better in time," said Mr. Billing. "Why, I wouldn't hurt a fly. I want to do good to people; not to hurt 'em. I'll have a pint," he added, turning to the bar.

"Not here you won't," said the landlord, eyeing him coldly.

"Why not?" demanded the astonished Mr. Billing.

"You've had all you ought to have already," was the reply. "And there's one thing I'll swear to—you ain't had it 'ere."

"I haven't 'ad a drop pass my lips began the outraged Mr. Billing.

"Yes, I know," said the other, wearily, as he shifted one or two glasses and wiped the counter; "I've heard it all before, over and over again. Mind you, I've been in this business thirty years, and if I don't know when a man's had his whack, and a drop more, nobody does. You get off 'ome and ask your missis to make you a nice cup o' good strong tea, and then get up to bed and sleep it off."

"I dare say," said Mr. Billing, with cold dignity, as he paused at the door—"I dare say I may give up beer altogether."

He stood outside pondering over the unforeseen difficulties attendant upon his new career, moving a few inches to one side as Mr. Ricketts, a foe of long standing, came towards the public-house, and, halting a yard or two away, eyed him warily.

"Come along," said Mr. Billing, speaking somewhat loudly, for the benefit of the men in the bar; "I sha'n't hurt you; my fighting days are over."

"Yes, I dessay," replied the other, edging away.

"It's all right, Bill," said a mutual friend, through the half-open door; "he's got a new 'art."

Mr. Ricketts looked perplexed. "'Art disease, d'ye mean?" he inquired, hopefully. "Can't he fight no more?"

"A new 'art," said Mr. Billing. "It's as strong as ever it was, but it's changed—brother."

"If you call me 'brother' agin I'll give you something for yourself, and chance it," said Mr. Ricketts, ferociously. "I'm a pore man, but I've got my pride."

Mr. Billing, with a smile charged with brotherly love, leaned his left cheek towards him. "Hit it," he said, gently.

"Give it a smack and run, Bill," said the voice of a well-wisher inside.

"There'd be no need for 'im to run," said Mr. Billing. "I wouldn't hit 'im back for anything. I should turn the other cheek."

"Whaffor?" inquired the amazed Mr. Ricketts.

"For another swipe," said Mr. Billing, radiantly.

In the fraction of a second he got the first, and reeled back staggering. The onlookers from the bar came out hastily. Mr. Ricketts, somewhat pale, stood his ground.

"You see, I don't hit you," said Mr. Billing, with a ghastly attempt at a smile.

He stood rubbing his cheek gently, and, remembering Mr. Purnip's statements, slowly, inch by inch, turned the other in the direction of his adversary. The circuit was still incomplete when Mr. Ricketts, balancing himself carefully, fetched it a smash that nearly burst it. Mr. Billing, somewhat jarred by his contact with the pavement, rose painfully and confronted him.

"I've only got two cheeks, mind," he said, slowly.

Mr. Ricketts sighed. "I wish you'd got a blinking dozen," he said, wistfully. "Well, so long. Be good."

He walked into the Blue Lion absolutely free from that sense of shame which Mr. Purnip had predicted, and, accepting a pint from an admirer, boasted noisily of his exploit. Mr. Billing, suffering both mentally and physically, walked slowly home to his astonished wife.

"P'r'aps he'll be ashamed of hisself when 'e comes to think it over," he murmured, as Mrs. Billing, rendered almost perfect by practice, administered first aid.

"I s'pect he's crying his eyes out," she said, with a sniff. "Tell me if that 'urts."

Mr. Billing told her, then, suddenly remembering himself, issued an expurgated edition.

"I'm sorry for the next man that 'its you," said his wife, as she drew back and regarded her handiwork.

"'Well, you needn't be," said Mr. Billing, with dignity. "It would take more than a couple o' props in the jaw to make me alter my mind when I've made it up. You ought to know that by this time. Hurry up and finish. I want you to go to the corner and fetch me a pot."

"What, ain't you going out agin?" demanded his astonished wife.

Mr. Billing shook his head. "Somebody else might want to give me one," he said, resignedly, "and I've 'ad about all I want to-night."

His face was still painful next morning, but as he sat at breakfast in the small kitchen he was able to refer to Mr. Ricketts in terms which were an eloquent testimony to Mr. Purnip's teaching. Mrs. Billing, unable to contain herself, wandered off into the front room with a duster.

"Are you nearly ready to go?" she inquired, returning after a short interval.

"Five minutes," said Mr. Billing, nodding. I'll just light my pipe and then I'm off."

"'Cos there's two or three waiting outside for you," added his wife.

Mr. Billing rose. "Ho, is there?" he said, grimly, as he removed his coat and proceeded to roll up his shirt-sleeves. "I'll learn 'em. I'll give 'em something to wait for. I'll—"

His voice died away as he saw the triumph in his wife's face, and, drawing down his sleeves again, he took up his coat and stood eyeing her in genuine perplexity.

"Tell 'em I've gorn," he said, at last.

"And what about telling lies?" demanded his wife. "What would your Mr. Purnip say to that?"

"You do as you're told," exclaimed the harassed Mr. Billing. "I'm not going to tell 'em; it's you."

Mrs. Billing returned to the parlour, and, with Mr. Billing lurking in the background, busied herself over a china flower-pot that stood in the window, and turned an anxious eye upon three men waiting outside. After a glance or two she went to the door.

"Did you want to see my husband?" she inquired.

The biggest of the three nodded. "Yus," he said, shortly.

"I'm sorry," said Mrs. Billing, "but he 'ad to go early this morning. Was it anything partikler?"

"Gorn?" said the other, in disappointed tones. "Well, you tell 'im I'll see 'im later on."

He turned away, and, followed by the other two, walked slowly up the road. Mr. Billing, after waiting till the coast was clear, went off in the other direction.

He sought counsel of his friend and mentor that afternoon, and stood beaming with pride at the praise lavished upon him. Mr. Purnip's co-workers were no less enthusiastic than their chief; and various suggestions were made to Mr. Billing as to his behaviour in the unlikely event of further attacks upon his noble person.

He tried to remember the suggestions in the harassing days that followed; baiting Joe Billing becoming popular as a pastime from which no evil results need be feared. It was creditable to his fellow-citizens that most of them refrained from violence with a man who declined to hit back, but as a butt his success was assured. The night when a gawky lad of eighteen drank up his beer, and then invited him to step outside if he didn't like it, dwelt long in his memory. And Elk Street thrilled one evening at the sight of their erstwhile champion flying up the road hotly pursued by a foeman half his size. His explanation to his indignant wife that, having turned the other cheek the night before, he was in no mood for further punishment, was received in chilling silence.

"They'll soon get tired of it," he said, hopefully; "and I ain't going to be beat by a lot of chaps wot I could lick with one 'and tied behind me. They'll get to understand in time; Mr. Purnip says so. It's a pity that you don't try and do some good yourself."

Mrs. Billing received the suggestion with a sniff; but the seed was sown. She thought the matter over in private, and came to the conclusion that, if her husband wished her to participate in good works, it was not for her to deny him. Hitherto her efforts in that direction had been promptly suppressed; Mr. Billing's idea being that if a woman looked after her home and her husband properly there should be neither time nor desire for anything else. His surprise on arriving home to tea on Saturday afternoon, and finding a couple of hard-working neighbours devouring his substance, almost deprived him of speech.

"Poor things," said his wife, after the guests had gone; "they did enjoy it. It's cheered 'em up wonderful. You and Mr. Purnip are quite right. I can see that now. You can tell him that it was you what put it into my 'art."

"Me? Why, I never dreamt o' such a thing," declared the surprised Mr. Billing. "And there's other ways of doing good besides asking a pack of old women in to tea."

"I know there is," said his wife. "All in good time," she added, with a far-away look in her eyes.

Mr. Billing cleared his throat, but nothing came of it. He cleared it again.

"I couldn't let you do all the good," said his wife, hastily. "It wouldn't be fair. I must help."

Mr. Billing lit his pipe noisily, and then took it out into the back-yard and sat down to think over the situation. The ungenerous idea that his wife was making goodness serve her own ends was the first that occurred to him.

His suspicions increased with time. Mrs. Billing's good works seemed to be almost entirely connected with hospitality. True, she had entertained Mr. Purnip and one of the ladies from the Settlement to tea, but that only riveted his bonds more firmly. Other visitors included his sister-in-law, for whom he had a great distaste, and some of the worst-behaved children in the street.

"It's only high spirits," said Mrs. Billing; "all children are like that. And I do it to help the mothers."

"And 'cos you like children," said her husband, preserving his good-humour with an effort.

There was a touch of monotony about the new life, and the good deeds that accompanied it, which, to a man of ardent temperament, was apt to pall. And Elk Street, instead of giving him the credit which was his due, preferred to ascribe the change in his behaviour to what they called being "a bit barmy on the crumpet."

He came home one evening somewhat dejected, brightening up as he stood in the passage and inhaled the ravishing odours from the kitchen. Mrs. Billing, with a trace of nervousness somewhat unaccountable in view of the excellent quality of the repast provided, poured him out a glass of beer, and passed flattering comment upon his appearance.

"Wot's the game?" he inquired.

"Game?" repeated his wife, in a trembling voice. "Nothing. 'Ow do you find that steak-pudding? I thought of giving you one every Wednesday."

Mr. Billing put down his knife and fork and sat regarding her thoughtfully. Then he pushed back his chair suddenly, and, a picture of consternation and wrath, held up his hand for silence.

"W-w-wot is it?" he demanded. "A cat?"

Mrs. Billing made no reply, and her husband sprang to his feet as a long, thin wailing sounded through the house. A note of temper crept into it and strengthened it.

"Wot is it?" demanded Mr. Billing again. "It's—it's Mrs. Smith's Charlie," stammered his wife.

"In—in my bedroom?" exclaimed her husband, in incredulous accents. "Wot's it doing there?"

"I took it for the night," said his wife hurriedly. "Poor thing, what with the others being ill she's 'ad a dreadful time, and she said if I'd take Charlie for a few—for a night, she might be able to get some sleep."

Mr. Billing choked. "And what about my sleep?" he shouted. "Chuck it outside at once. D'ye hear me?"

His words fell on empty air, his wife having already sped upstairs to pacify Master Smith by a rhythmical and monotonous thumping on the back. Also she lifted up a thin and not particularly sweet voice and sang to him. Mr. Billing, finishing his supper in indignant silence, told himself grimly that he was "beginning to have enough of it."

He spent the evening at the Charlton Arms, and, returning late, went slowly and heavily up to bed. In the light of a shaded candle he saw a small, objectionable-looking infant fast asleep on two chairs by the side of the bed.

"H'sh!" said his wife, in a thrilling whisper. "He's just gone off."

"D'ye mean I mustn't open my mouth in my own bedroom?" demanded the indignant man, loudly.

"H'sh!" said his wife again.

It was too late. Master Smith, opening first one eye and then the other, finished by opening his mouth. The noise was appalling.

"H'sh! H'sh!" repeated Mrs. Billing, as her husband began to add to the noise. "Don't wake 'im right up."

"Right up?" repeated the astonished man. "Right up? Why, is he doing this in 'is sleep?"

He subsided into silence, and, undressing with stealthy care, crept into bed and lay there, marvelling at his self-control. He was a sound sleeper, but six times at least he was awakened by Mrs. Billing slipping out of bed—regardless of draughts to her liege lord—and marching up and down the room with the visitor in her arms. He rose in the morning and dressed in ominous silence.

"I 'ope he didn't disturb you," said his wife, anxiously.

"You've done it," replied Mr. Billing. "You've upset everything now. Since I joined the Purnip lot everybody's took advantage of me; now I'm going to get some of my own back. You wouldn't ha' dreamt of behaving like this a few weeks ago."

"Oh, Joe!" said his wife, entreatingly; "and everybody's been so happy!"

"Except me," retorted Joe Billing. "You come down and get my breakfast ready. If I start early I shall catch Mr. Bill Ricketts on 'is way to work. And mind, if I find that steam-orgin 'ere when I come 'ome to-night you'll hear of it."

He left the house with head erect and the light of battle in his eyes, and, meeting Mr. Ricketts at the corner, gave that justly aggrieved gentleman the surprise of his life. Elk Street thrilled to the fact that Mr. Billing had broken out again, and spoke darkly of what the evening might bring forth. Curious eyes followed his progress as he returned home from work, and a little later on the news was spread abroad that he was out and paying off old scores with an ardour that nothing could withstand.

"And wot about your change of 'art?" demanded one indignant matron, as her husband reached home five seconds ahead of Mr. Billing and hid in the scullery.

"It's changed agin," said Mr. Billing, simply.

He finished the evening in the Blue Lion, where he had one bar almost to himself, and, avoiding his wife's reproachful glance when he arrived home, procured some warm water and began to bathe his honourable scars.

"Mr. Purnip 'as been round with another gentleman," said his wife.

Mr. Billing said, "Oh!"

"Very much upset they was, and 'ope you'll go and see them," she continued.

Mr. Billing said "Oh!" again; and, after thinking the matter over, called next day at the Settlement and explained his position.

"It's all right for gentlemen like you," he said civilly. "But a man. like me can't call his soul 'is own—or even 'is bedroom. Everybody takes advantage of 'im. Nobody ever gives you a punch, and, as for putting babies in your bedroom, they wouldn't dream of it."

He left amid expressions of general regret, turning a deaf ear to all suggestions about making another start, and went off exulting in his freedom.

His one trouble was Mr. Purnip, that estimable gentleman, who seemed to have a weird gift of meeting him at all sorts of times and places, never making any allusion to his desertion, but showing quite clearly by his manner that he still hoped for the return of the wanderer. It was awkward for a man of sensitive disposition, and Mr. Billing, before entering a street, got into the habit of peering round the corner first.

He pulled up suddenly one evening as he saw his tenacious friend, accompanied by a lady-member, some little distance ahead. Then he sprang forward with fists clenched as a passer-by, after scowling at Mr. Purnip, leaned forward and deliberately blew a mouthful of smoke into the face of his companion.

Mr. Billing stopped again and stood gaping with astonishment. The aggressor was getting up from the pavement, while Mr. Purnip, in an absolutely correct attitude, stood waiting for him. Mr. Billing in a glow of delight edged forward, and, with a few other fortunates, stood by watching one of the best fights that had ever been seen in the district. Mr. Purnip's foot-work was excellent, and the way he timed his blows made Mr. Billing's eyes moist with admiration.

It was over at last. The aggressor went limping off, and Mr. Purnip, wiping his bald head, picked up his battered and dusty hat from the roadway and brushed it on his sleeve. He turned with a start and a blush to meet the delighted gaze of Mr. Billing.

"I'm ashamed of myself," he murmured, brokenly—"ashamed."

"Ashamed !" exclaimed the amazed Mr. Billing. "Why, a pro couldn't ha' done better."

"Such an awful example," moaned the other. "All my good work here thrown away."

"Don't you believe it, sir," said Mr. Billing, earnestly. "As soon as this gets about you'll get more members than you want a'most. I'm coming back, for one."

Mr. Purnip turned and grasped his hand.

"I understand things now," said Mr. Billing, nodding sagely. "Turning the other cheek's all right so long as you don't do it always. If you don't let 'em know whether you are going to turn the other cheek or knock their blessed heads off, it's all right. 'Arf the trouble in the world is caused by letting people know too much."

THE COOK OF THE "GANNET"

All ready for sea, and no cook," said the mate of the schooner Gannet, gloomily. "What's become of all the cooks I can't think."

"They most on 'em ship as mates now," said the skipper, grinning. "But you needn't worry about that; I've got one coming aboard to-night. I'm trying a new experiment, George."

"I once knew a chemist who tried one," said George, "an' it blew him out of the winder; but I never heard o' shipmasters trying 'em."

"There's all kinds of experiments," rejoined the other, "What do you say to a lady cook, George?"

"A WHAT?" asked the mate in tones of strong amazement. "What, aboard a schooner?"

"Why not?" inquired the skipper warmly; "why not? There's plenty of 'em ashore—why not aboard ship?"

"'Tain't proper, for one thing," said the mate virtuously.

"I shouldn't have expected you to have thought o' that," said the other unkindly. "Besides, they have stewardesses on big ships, an' what's the difference? She's a sort o' relation o' mine, too—cousin o' my wife's, a widder woman, and a good sensible age, an' as the doctor told her to take a sea voyage for the benefit of her 'elth, she's coming with me for six months as cook. She'll take her meals with us; but, o' course, the men are not to know of the relationship."

"What about sleeping accommodation?" inquired the mate, with the air of a man putting a poser.

"I've thought o' that," replied the other; "it's all arranged."

The mate, with an uncompromising air, waited for information.

"She—she's to have your berth, George," continued the skipper, without looking at him. "You can have that nice, large, airy locker."

"One what the biscuit and onions kep' in?" inquired George.

The skipper nodded.

"I think, if it's all the same to you," said the mate, with laboured politeness, "I'll wait till the butter keg's empty, and crowd into that."

"It's no use your making yourself unpleasant about it," said the skipper, "not a bit. The arrangements are made now, and here she comes."

Following his gaze, the mate looked up as a stout, comely-looking woman of middle age came along the jetty, followed by the watchman staggering under a box of enormous proportions.

"Jim!" cried the lady.

"Halloa!" cried the skipper, starting uneasily at the title. "We've been expecting you for some time."

"There's a row on with the cabman," said the lady calmly. "This silly old man"—the watchman snorted fiercely—"let the box go through the window getting it off the top, and the cabman wants ME to pay. He's out there using language, and he keeps calling me grandma—I want you to have him locked up."

"Come down below now," said the skipper; "we'll see about the cab. Mrs. Blossom—my mate. George, go and send that cab away."

Mrs. Blossom, briefly acknowledging the introduction, followed the skipper to the cabin, while the mate, growling under his breath, went out to enter into a verbal contest in which he was from the first hopelessly overmatched.

The new cook, being somewhat fatigued with her journey, withdrew at an early hour, and the sun was well up when she appeared on deck next morning. The wharves and warehouses of the night before had disappeared, and the schooner, under a fine spread of canvas, was just passing Tilbury.

"There's one thing I must put a stop to," said the skipper, as he and the mate, after an admirably-cooked breakfast, stood together talking. "The men seem to be hanging round that galley too much."

"What can you expect?" demanded the mate. "They've all got their Sunday clothes on too, pretty dears."

"Hi, you Bill!" cried the skipper. "What are you doing there?"

"Lending cook a hand with the saucepans, sir," said Bill, an oakum-bearded man of sixty.

"There ain't no call for 'im to come 'ere at all, sir," shouted another seaman, putting his head out of the galley. "Me an' cook's lifting 'em beautiful."

"Come out, both of you, or I'll start you with a rope!" roared the irritated commander.

"What's the matter?" inquired Mrs. Blossom. "They're not doing any harm."

"I can't have 'em there," said the skipper gruffly. "They've got other things to do."

"I must have some assistance with that boiler and the saucepans," said Mrs. Blossom decidedly, "so don't you interfere with what don't concern you, Jimmy."

"That's mutiny," whispered the horrified mate. "Sheer, rank mutiny."

"She don't know no better," whispered the other back. "Cook, you mustn't talk like that to the cap'n—what me and the mate tell you you must do. You don't understand yet, but it'll come easier by-and-bye."

"WILL it," demanded Mrs. Blossom loudly; "WILL it? I don't think it will. How dare you talk to me like that, Jim Harris? You ought to be ashamed of yourself!"

"My name's Cap'n Harris," said the skipper stiffly.

"Well, CAPTAIN Harris," said Mrs. Blossom scornfully; "and what'll happen if I don't do as you and that other shamefaced-looking man tell me?"

"We hope it won't come to that," said Harris, with quiet dignity, as he paused at the companion. "But the mate's in charge just now, and I warn you he's a very severe man. Don't stand no nonsense, George."

With these brave words the skipper disappeared below, and the mate, after one glance at the dauntless and imposing attitude of Mrs. Blossom, walked to the side and became engrossed in a passing steamer. A hum of wondering admiration arose from the crew, and the cook, thoroughly satisfied with her victory, returned to the scene of her labours.

For the next twenty-four hours Mrs. Blossom reigned supreme, and performed the cooking for the vessel, assisted by five ministering seamen. The weather was fine, and the wind light, and the two officers were at their wits' end to find jobs for the men.

"Why don't you put your foot down," grumbled the mate, as a burst of happy laughter came from the direction of the galley. "The idea of men laughing like that aboard ship; they're carrying on just as though we wasn't here."

"Will you stand by me?" demanded the skipper, pale but determined.

"Of course I will," said the other indignantly.

"Now, my lads," said Harris, stepping forward, "I can't have you chaps hanging round the galley all day; you're getting in cook's way and hindering her. Just get your knives out; I'll have the masts scraped."

"You just stay where you are," said Mrs. Blossom. "When they're in my way, I'll soon let 'em know."

"Did you hear what I said?" thundered the skipper, as the men hesitated.

"Aye, aye, sir," muttered the crew, moving off.

"How dare you interfere with me?" said Mrs. Blossom hotly, as she realised the defeat. "Ever since I've been on this ship you've been trying to aggravate me. I wonder the men don't hit you, you nasty, ginger-whiskered little man."

"Go on with your work," said the skipper, fondly stroking the maligned whiskers.

"Don't you talk to me, Jim Harris," said Mrs. Blossom, quivering with wrath. "Don't you give ME none of your airs. WHO BORROWED FIVE POUNDS **FROM MY POOR DEAD HUSBAND JUST BEFORE HE DIED, AND NEVER PAID IT BACK?**"

"Go on with your work," repeated the skipper, with pale lips.

"WHOSE UNCLE BENJAMIN HAD THREE WEEKS?" demanded Mrs. Blossom darkly. **"WHOSE UNCLE JOSEPH HAD TO GO ABROAD WITHOUT STOPPING TO PACK UP?"**

The skipper made no reply, but the anxiety of the crew to have these vital problems solved was so manifest that he turned his back on the virago and went towards the mate, who at that moment dipped hurriedly to escape a wet dish-clout. The two men regarded each other, pale with anxiety.

"Now, you just move off," said Mrs. Blossom, shaking another clout at them. "I won't have you hanging about my galley. Keep to your own end of the ship."

The skipper drew himself up haughtily, but the effect was somewhat marred by one eye, which dwelt persistently on the clout, and after a short inward struggle he moved off, accompanied by the mate. Wellington himself would have been nonplussed by a wet cloth in the hands of a fearless woman.

"She'll just have to have her own way till we get to Llanelly," said the indignant skipper, "and then I'll send her home by train and ship another cook. I knew she'd got a temper, but I didn't know it was like this. She's the last woman that sets foot on my ship—that's all she's done for her sex."

In happy ignorance of her impending doom Mrs. Blossom went blithely about her duties, assisted by a crew whose admiration for her increased by leaps and bounds; and the only thing which ventured to interfere with her was a stiff Atlantic roll, which they encountered upon rounding the Land's End.

The first intimation Mrs. Blossom had of it was the falling of small utensils in the galley. After she had picked them up and replaced them several times, she went out to investigate, and discovered that the schooner was dipping her bows to big green waves, and rolling, with much straining and creaking, from side to side. A fine spray, which broke over the bows and flew over the vessel, drove her back into the galley, which had suddenly developed an unaccountable stuffiness; but, though the crew to a man advised her to lie down and have a cup of tea, she repelled them with scorn, and with pale face and compressed lips stuck to her post.

Two days later they made fast to the quay at Llanelly, and half-an-hour later the skipper called the mate down to the cabin, and, handing him some money, told him to pay the cook off and ship another. The mate declined.

"You obey orders," said the skipper fiercely, "else you an' me'll quarrel."

"I've got a wife an' family," urged the mate.

"Pooh!" said the skipper. "Rubbish!"

"And uncles," added the mate rebelliously.

"Very good," said the skipper, glaring. "We'll ship the other cook first and let him settle it. After all, I don't see why we should fight his battles for him."

The mate, being agreeable, went off at once; and when Mrs. Blossom, after a little shopping ashore, returned to the Gannet she found the galley in the possession of one of the fattest cooks that ever broke ship's biscuit.

"Hullo!" said she, realising the situation at a glance, "what are you doing here?"

"Cooking," said the other gruffly. Then, catching sight of his questioner, he smiled amorously and winked at her.

"Don't you wink at me," said Mrs. Blossom wrathfully. "Come out of that galley."

"There's room for both," said the new cook persuasively. "Come in an' put your 'ed on my shoulder."

Utterly unprepared for this mode of attack, Mrs. Blossom lost her nerve, and, instead of storming the galley, as she had fully intended, drew back and retired to the cabin, where she found a short note from the skipper, enclosing her pay, and requesting her to take the train home. After reading this she went ashore again, returning presently with a big bundle, which she placed on the cabin table in front of Harris and the mate, who had just begun tea.

"I'm not going home by train," said she, opening the bundle, which contained a spirit kettle and provisions. "I'm going back with you; but I am not going to be beholden to you for anything—I 'm going to board myself."

After this declaration she made herself tea and sat down. The meal proceeded in silence, though occasionally she astonished her companions by little mysterious laughs, which caused them slight uneasiness. As she made no hostile demonstration, however, they became reassured, and congratulated themselves upon the success of their manoeuvre.

"How long shall we be getting back to London, do you think?" inquired Mrs. Blossom at last.

"We shall probably sail Tuesday night, and it may be anything from six days upwards," answered the skipper. "If this wind holds it'll probably be upwards."

To his great concern Mrs. Blossom put her handkerchief over her face, and, shaking with suppressed laughter, rose from the table and left the cabin.

The couple left eyed each other wonderingly.

"Did I say anything pertickler funny, George?" inquired the skipper, after some deliberation.

"Didn't strike me so," said the mate carelessly; "I expect she's thought o' something else to say about your family. She wouldn't be so good-tempered as all that for nothing. I feel cur'ous to know what it is."

"If you paid more attention to your own business," said the skipper, his choler rising, "you'd get on better. A mate who was a good seaman wouldn't ha' let a cook go on like this—it's not discipline."

He went off in dudgeon, and a coolness sprang up between them, which lasted until the bustle of starting in the small hours of Wednesday morning.

Once under way the day passed uneventfully, the schooner crawling sluggishly down the coast of Wales, and, when the skipper turned in that night, it was with the pleasant conviction that Mrs. Blossom had shot her last bolt, and, like a sensible woman, was going to accept her defeat. From this pleasing idea he was aroused suddenly by the watch stamping heavily on the deck overhead.

"What's up?" cried the skipper, darting up the companion-ladder, jostled by the mate.

"I dunno," said Bill, who was at the wheel, shakily. "Mrs. Blossom come up on deck a little while ago, and since then there's been three or four heavy splashes."

"She can't have gone overboard," said the skipper, in tones to which he manfully strove to impart a semblance of anxiety. "No, here she is. Anything wrong, Mrs. Blossom?"

"Not so far as I'm concerned," replied the lady, passing him and going below.

"You've been dreaming, Bill," said the skipper sharply.

"I ain't," said Bill stoutly. "I tell you I heard splashes. It's my belief she coaxed the cook up on deck, and then shoved him overboard. A woman could do anything with a man like that cook."

"I'll soon see," said the mate, and walking forward he put his head down the fore-scuttle and yelled for the cook.

"Aye, aye, sir," answered a voice sleepily, while the other men started up in their bunks. "Do you want me?"

"Bill thinks somebody has gone overboard," said the mate. "Are you all here?"

In answer to this the mystified men turned out all standing, and came on deck yawning and rubbing their eyes, while the mate explained the situation. Before he had finished the cook suddenly darted off to the galley, and the next moment the forlorn cry of a bereaved soul broke on their startled ears.

"What is it?" cried the mate.

"Come here!" shouted the cook, "look at this!"

He struck a match and held it aloft in his shaking fingers, and the men, who were worked up to a great pitch of excitement and expected to see something ghastly, after staring hard for some time in vain, profanely requested him to be more explicit.

"She's thrown all the saucepans and things overboard," said the cook with desperate calmness. "This lid of a tea kettle is all that's left for me to do the cooking in."

The Gannet, manned by seven famine-stricken misogynists, reached London six days later, the skipper obstinately refusing to put in at an intermediate port to replenish his stock of hardware. The most he would consent to do was to try and borrow from a passing vessel, but the unseemly behaviour of the master of a brig, who lost two hours owing to their efforts to obtain a saucepan of him, utterly discouraged any further attempts in that direction, and they settled down to a diet of biscuits and water, and salt beef scorched on the stove.

Mrs. Blossom, unwilling perhaps to witness their sufferings, remained below, and when they reached London, only consented to land under the supervision of a guard of honour, composed of all the able-bodied men on the wharf.

CUPBOARD LOVE

In the comfortable living-room at Negget's farm, half parlour and half kitchen, three people sat at tea in the waning light of a November afternoon. Conversation, which had been brisk, had languished somewhat, owing to Mrs. Negget glancing at frequent intervals toward the door, behind which she was convinced the servant was listening, and checking the finest periods and the most startling suggestions with a warning 'ssh!

"Go on, uncle," she said, after one of these interruptions.

"I forget where I was," said Mr. Martin Bodfish, shortly.

"Under our bed," Mr. Negget reminded him.

"Yes, watching," said Mrs. Negget, eagerly.

It was an odd place for an ex-policeman, especially as a small legacy added to his pension had considerably improved his social position, but Mr. Bodfish had himself suggested it in the professional hope that the person who had taken Mrs. Negget's gold brooch might try for further loot. He had, indeed, suggested baiting the dressing-table with the farmer's watch, an idea which Mr. Negget had promptly vetoed.

"I can't help thinking that Mrs. Pottle knows something about it," said Mrs. Negget, with an indignant glance at her husband.

"Mrs. Pottle," said the farmer, rising slowly and taking a seat on the oak settle built in the fireplace, "has been away from the village for near a fortnit."

"I didn't say she took it," snapped his wife. "I said I believe she knows something about it, and so I do. She's a horrid woman. Look at the way she encouraged her girl Looey to run after that young traveller from Smithson's. The whole fact of the matter is, it isn't your brooch, so you don't care."

"I said—" began Mr. Negget.

"I know what you said," retorted his wife, sharply, "and I wish you'd be quiet and not interrupt uncle. Here's my uncle been in the police twenty-five years, and you won't let him put a word in edgeways.'

"My way o' looking at it," said the ex-policeman, slowly, "is different to that o' the law; my idea is, an' always has been, that everybody is guilty until they've proved their innocence."

"It's a wonderful thing to me," said Mr. Negget in a low voice to his pipe, "as they should come to a house with a retired policeman living in it. Looks to me like somebody that ain't got much respect for the police."

The ex-policeman got up from the table, and taking a seat on the settle opposite the speaker, slowly filled a long clay and took a spill from the fireplace. His pipe lit, he turned to his niece, and slowly bade her go over the account of her loss once more.

"I missed it this morning," said Mrs. Negget, rapidly, "at ten minutes past twelve o'clock by the clock, and half-past five by my watch which wants looking to. I'd just put the batch of bread into the oven, and gone upstairs and opened the box that stands on my drawers to get a lozenge, and I missed the brooch."

"Do you keep it in that box?" asked the ex-policeman, slowly.

"Always," replied his niece. "I at once came down stairs and told Emma that the brooch had been stolen. I said that I named no names, and didn't wish to think bad of anybody, and that if I found the brooch back in the box when I went up stairs again, I should forgive whoever took it."

"And what did Emma say?" inquired Mr. Bodfish.

"Emma said a lot o' things," replied Mrs. Negget, angrily. "I'm sure by the lot she had to say you'd ha' thought she was the missis and me the servant. I gave her a month's notice at once, and she went straight up stairs and sat on her box and cried."

"Sat on her box?" repeated the ex-constable, impressively. "Oh!"

"That's what I thought," said his niece, "but it wasn't, because I got her off at last and searched it through and through. I never saw anything like her clothes in all my life. There was hardly a button or a tape on; and as for her stockings—"

"She don't get much time," said Mr. Negget, slowly.

"That's right; I thought you'd speak up for her," cried his wife, shrilly.

"Look here—" began Mr. Negget, laying his pipe on the seat by his side and rising slowly.

"Keep to the case in hand," said the ex-constable, waving him back to his seat again. "Now, Lizzie."

"I searched her box through and through," said his niece, "but it wasn't there; then I came down again and had a rare good cry all to myself."

"That's the best way for you to have it," remarked Mr. Negget, feelingly.

Mrs. Negget's uncle instinctively motioned his niece to silence, and holding his chin in his hand, scowled frightfully in the intensity of thought.

"See a cloo?" inquired Mr. Negget, affably.

"You ought to be ashamed of yourself, George," said his wife, angrily; "speaking to uncle when he's looking like that."

Mr. Bodfish said nothing; it is doubtful whether he even heard these remarks; but he drew a huge notebook from his pocket, and after vainly trying to point his pencil by suction, took a knife from the table and hastily sharpened it.

"Was the brooch there last night?" he inquired.

"It were," said Mr. Negget, promptly. "Lizzie made me get up just as the owd clock were striking twelve to get her a lozenge."

"It seems pretty certain that the brooch went since then," mused Mr. Bodfish.

"It would seem like it to a plain man," said Mr. Negget, guardedly.

"I should like to see the box," said Mr. Bodfish.

Mrs. Negget went up and fetched it and stood eyeing him eagerly as he raised the lid and inspected the contents. It contained only a few lozenges and some bone studs. Mr. Negget helped himself to a lozenge, and going back to his seat, breathed peppermint.

"Properly speaking, that ought not to have been touched," said the ex-constable, regarding him with some severity.

"Eh!" said the startled farmer, putting his finger to his lips.

"Never mind," said the other, shaking his head. "It's too late now."

"He doesn't care a bit," said Mrs. Negget, somewhat sadly. "He used to keep buttons in that box with the lozenges until one night he gave me one by mistake. Yes, you may laugh—I'm glad you can laugh."

Mr. Negget, feeling that his mirth was certainly ill-timed, shook for some time in a noble effort to control himself, and despairing at length, went into the back place to recover. Sounds of blows indicative of Emma slapping him on the back did not add to Mrs. Negget's serenity.

"The point is," said the ex-constable, "could anybody have come into your room while you was asleep and taken it?"

"No," said Mrs. Negget, decisively. I'm a very poor sleeper, and I'd have woke at once, but if a flock of elephants was to come in the room they wouldn't wake George. He'd sleep through anything."

"Except her feeling under my piller for her handkerchief," corroborated Mr. Negget, returning to the sitting-room.

Mr. Bodfish waved them to silence, and again gave way to deep thought. Three times he took up his pencil, and laying it down again, sat and drummed on the table with his fingers. Then he arose, and with bent head walked slowly round and round the room until he stumbled over a stool.

"Nobody came to the house this morning, I suppose?" he said at length, resuming his seat.

"Only Mrs. Driver," said his niece.

"What time did she come?" inquired Mr. Bodfish.

"Here! look here!" interposed Mr. Negget. "I've known Mrs. Driver thirty year a'most."

"What time did she come?" repeated the ex-constable, pitilessly.

His niece shook her head. "It might have been eleven, and again it might have been earlier," she replied. "I was out when she came."

"Out!" almost shouted the other.

Mrs. Negget nodded.

"She was sitting in here when I came back."

Her uncle looked up and glanced at the door behind which a small staircase led to the room above.

"What was to prevent Mrs. Driver going up there while you were away?" he demanded.

"I shouldn't like to think that of Mrs. Driver," said his niece, shaking her head; "but then in these days one never knows what might happen. Never. I've given up thinking about it. However, when I came back, Mrs. Driver was here, sitting in that very chair you are sitting in now."

Mr. Bodfish pursed up his lips and made another note. Then he took a spill from the fireplace, and lighting a candle, went slowly and carefully up the stairs. He found nothing on them but two caked rims of mud, and being too busy to notice Mr. Negget's frantic signalling, called his niece's attention to them.

"What do you think of that?" he demanded, triumphantly.

"Somebody's been up there," said his niece. "It isn't Emma, because she hasn't been outside the house all day; and it can't be George, because he promised me faithful he'd never go up there in his dirty boots."

Mr. Negget coughed, and approaching the stairs, gazed with the eye of a stranger at the relics as Mr. Bodfish hotly rebuked a suggestion of his niece's to sweep them up.

"Seems to me," said the conscience-stricken Mr. Negget, feebly, "as they're rather large for a woman."

"Mud cakes," said Mr. Bodfish, with his most professional manner; "a small boot would pick up a lot this weather."

"So it would," said Mr. Negget, and with brazen effrontery not only met his wife's eye without quailing, but actually glanced down at her boots.

Mr. Bodfish came back to his chair and ruminated. Then he looked up and spoke.

"It was missed this morning at ten minutes past twelve," he said, slowly; "it was there last night. At eleven o'clock you came in and found Mrs. Driver sitting in that chair."

"No, the one you're in," interrupted his niece.

"It don't signify," said her uncle. "Nobody else has been near the place, and Emma's box has been searched."

"Thoroughly searched," testified Mrs. Negget.

"Now the point is, what did Mrs. Driver come for this morning?" resumed the ex-constable. "Did she come—"

He broke off and eyed with dignified surprise a fine piece of wireless telegraphy between husband and wife. It appeared that Mr. Negget sent off a humorous message with his left eye, the right being for some reason closed, to which Mrs. Negget replied with a series of frowns and staccato shakes of the head, which her husband found easily translatable. Under the austere stare of Mr. Bodfish their faces at once regained their wonted calm, and the ex-constable in a somewhat offended manner resumed his inquiries.

"Mrs. Driver has been here a good bit lately," he remarked, slowly.

Mr. Negget's eyes watered, and his mouth worked piteously.

"If you can't behave yourself, George—began began his wife, fiercely.

"What is the matter?" demanded Mr. Bodfish. "I'm not aware that I've said anything to be laughed at."

"No more you have, uncle," retorted his niece; "only George is such a stupid. He's got an idea in his silly head that Mrs. Driver—But it's all nonsense, of course."

"I've merely got a bit of an idea that it's a wedding-ring, not a brooch, Mrs. Driver is after," said the farmer to the perplexed constable.

Mr. Bodfish looked from one to the other. "But you always keep yours on, Lizzie, don't you?" he asked.

"Yes, of course," replied his niece, hurriedly; "but George has always got such strange ideas. Don't take no notice of him."

Her uncle sat back in his chair, his face still wrinkled perplexedly; then the wrinkles vanished sudden y, chased away by a huge glow, and he rose wrathfully and towered over the match-making Mr. Negget. "How dare you?" he gasped.

Mr. Negget made no reply, but in a cowardly fashion jerked his thumb toward his wife.

"Oh! George! How can you say so?" said the latter.

"I should never ha' thought of it by myself," said the farmer; "but I think they'd make a very nice couple, and I'm sure Mrs. Driver thinks so."

The ex-constable sat down in wrathful confusion, and taking up his notebook again, watched over the top of it the silent charges and countercharges of his niece and her husband.

"If I put my finger on the culprit," he asked at length, turning to his niece, "what do you wish done to her?"

Mrs. Negget regarded him with an expression which contained all the Christian virtues rolled into one.

"Nothing," she said, softly. "I only want my brooch back."

The ex-constable shook his head at this leniency.

"Well, do as you please," he said, slowly. "In the first place, I want you to ask Mrs. Driver here to tea to-morrow—oh, I don't mind Negget's ridiculous ideas—pity he hasn't got something better to think of; if she's guilty, I'll soon find it out. I'll play with her like a cat with a mouse. I'll make her convict herself."

"Look here!" said Mr. Negget, with sudden vigour. "I won't have it. I won't have no woman asked here to tea to be got at like that. There's only my friends comes here to tea, and if any friend stole anything o' mine, I'd be one o' the first to hush it up."

"If they were all like you, George," said his wife, angrily, "where would the law be?"

"Or the police?" demanded Mr. Bodfish, staring at him.

"I won't have it!" repeated the farmer, loudly. "I'm the law here, and I'm the police here. That little tiny bit o' dirt was off my boots, I dare say. I don't care if it was."

"Very good," said Mr. Bodfish, turning to his indignant niece; "if he likes to look at it that way, there's nothing more to be said. I only wanted to get your brooch back for you, that's all; but if he's against it—"

"I'm against your asking Mrs. Driver here to my house to be got at," said the farmer.

"O' course if you can find out who took the brooch, and get it back again anyway, that's another matter."

Mr. Bodfish leaned over the table toward his niece.

"If I get an opportunity, I'll search her cottage," he said, in a low voice. "Strictly speaking, it ain't quite a legal thing to do, o course, but many o' the finest pieces of detective work have been done by breaking the law. If she's a kleptomaniac, it's very likely lying about somewhere in the house."

He eyed Mr. Negget closely, as though half expecting another outburst, but none being forthcoming, sat back in his chair again and smoked in silence, while Mrs. Negget, with a carpet-brush which almost spoke, swept the pieces of dried mud from the stairs.

Mr. Negget was the last to go to bed that night, and finishing his pipe over the dying fire, sat for some time in deep thought. He had from the first raised objections to the presence of Mr. Bodfish at the farm, but family affection, coupled with an idea of testamentary benefits, had so wrought with his wife that he had allowed her to have her own way. Now he half fancied that he saw a chance of getting rid of him. If he could only enable the widow to catch him searching her house, it was highly probable that the ex-constable would find the village somewhat too hot to hold him. He gave his right leg a congratulatory slap as he thought of it, and knocking the ashes from his pipe, went slowly up to bed.

He was so amiable next morning that Mr. Bodfish, who was trying to explain to Mrs. Negget the difference between theft and kleptomania, spoke before him freely. The ex-constable defined kleptomania as a sort of amiable weakness found chiefly among the upper circles, and cited the case of a lady of title whose love of diamonds, combined with great hospitality, was a source of much embarrassment to her guests.

For the whole of that day Mr. Bodfish hung about in the neighbourhood of the widow's cottage, but in vain, and it would be hard to say whether he or Mr. Negget, who had been discreetly shadowing him, felt the disappointment most. On the day following, however, the ex-constable from a distant hedge saw a friend of the widow's enter the cottage, and a little later both ladies emerged and walked up the road.

He watched them turn the corner, and then, with a cautious glance round, which failed, however, to discover Mr. Negget, the ex-constable strolled casually in the direction of the cottage, and approaching it from the rear, turned the handle of the door and slipped in.

He searched the parlour hastily, and then, after a glance from the window, ventured up stairs. And he was in the thick of his self-imposed task when his graceless nephew by marriage, who had met Mrs. Driver and referred pathetically to a raging thirst which he had hoped to have quenched with some of her home-brewed, brought the ladies hastily back again.

"I'll go round the back way," said the wily Negget as they approached the cottage. "I just want to have a look at that pig of yours."

He reached the back door at the same time as Mr. Bodfish, and placing his legs apart, held it firmly against the frantic efforts of the exconstable. The struggle ceased suddenly, and the door opened easily just as Mrs. Driver and her friend appeared in the front room, and the farmer, with a keen glance at the door of the larder which had just closed, took a chair while his hostess drew a glass of beer from the barrel in the kitchen.

Mr. Negget drank gratefully and praised the brew. From beer the conversation turned naturally to the police, and from the police to the listening Mr. Bodfish, who was economizing space by sitting on the bread-pan, and trembling with agitation.

"He's a lonely man," said Negget, shaking his head and glancing from the corner of his eye at the door of the larder. In his wildest dreams he had not imagined so choice a position, and he resolved to give full play to an idea which suddenly occurred to him.

"I dare say," said Mrs. Driver, carelessly, conscious that her friend was watching her.

"And the heart of a little child," said Negget; "you wouldn't believe how simple he is."

Mrs. Clowes said that it did him credit, but, speaking for herself, she hadn't noticed it.

"He was talking about you night before last," said Negget, turning to his hostess; "not that that's anything fresh. He always is talking about you nowadays."

The widow coughed confusedly and told him not to be foolish.

"Ask my wife," said the farmer, impressively; "they were talking about you for hours. He's a very shy man is my wife's uncle, but you should see his face change when your name's mentioned."

As a matter of fact, Mr. Bodfish's face was at that very moment taking on a deeper shade of crimson.

"Everything you do seems to interest him," continued the farmer, disregarding Mrs. Driver's manifest distress; "he was asking Lizzie about your calling on Monday; how long you stayed, and where you sat; and after she'd told him, I'm blest if he didn't go and sit in the same chair!"

This romantic setting to a perfectly casual action on the part of Mr. Bodfish affected the widow visibly, but its effect on the ex-constable nearly upset the bread-pan.

"But here," continued Mr. Negget, with another glance at the larder, "he might go on like that for years. He's a wunnerful shy man—big, and gentle, and shy. He wanted Lizzie to ask you to tea yesterday."

"Now, Mr. Negget," said the blushing widow. "Do be quiet."

"Fact," replied the farmer; "solemn fact, I assure you. And he asked her whether you were fond of jewellery."

"I met him twice in the road near here yesterday," said Mrs. Clowes, suddenly. "Perhaps he was waiting for you to come out."

"I dare say," replied the farmer. "I shouldn't wonder but what he's hanging about somewhere near now, unable to tear himself away."

Mr. Bodfish wrung his hands, and his thoughts reverted instinctively to instances in his memory in which charges of murder had been altered by the direction of a sensible judge to manslaughter. He held his breath for the next words.

Mr. Negget drank a little more ale and looked at Mrs. Driver.

"I wonder whether you've got a morsel of bread and cheese?" he said, slowly. "I've come over that hungry—"

The widow and Mr. Bodfish rose simultaneously. It required not the brain of a trained detective to know that the cheese was in the larder. The unconscious Mrs. Driver opened the door, and then with a wild scream fell back before the emerging form of Mr. Bodfish into the arms of Mrs. Clowes. The glass of Mr. Negget smashed on the floor, and the farmer himself, with every appearance of astonishment, stared at the apparition open-mouthed.

"Mr.—Bodfish!" he said at length, slowly.

Mr. Bodfish, incapable of speech, glared at him ferociously.

"Leave him alone," said Mrs. Clowes, who was ministering to her friend. "Can't you see the man's upset at frightening her? She's coming round, Mr. Bodfish; don't be alarmed."

"Very good," said the farmer, who found his injured relative's gaze somewhat trying. "I'll go, and leave him to explain to Mrs. Driver why he was hidden in her larder. It don't seem a proper thing to me."

"Why, you silly man," said Mrs. Clowes, gleefully, as she paused at the door, "that don't want any explanation. Now, Mr. Bodfish, we're giving you your chance. Mind you make the most of it, and don't be too shy."

She walked excitedly up the road with the farmer, and bidding him good-bye at the corner, went off hastily to spread the news. Mr. Negget walked home soberly, and hardly staying long enough to listen to his wife's account of the finding of the brooch between the chest of drawers and the wall, went off to spend the evening with a friend, and ended by making a night of it.

DESERTED

"Sailormen ain't wot you might call dandyfied as a rule," said the night-watchman, who had just had a passage of arms with a lighterman and been advised to let somebody else wash him and make a good job of it; "they've got too much sense. They leave dressing up and making eyesores of theirselves to men wot 'ave never smelt salt water; men wot drift up and down the river in lighters and get in everybody's way."

He glanced fiercely at the retreating figure of the lighterman, and, turning a deaf ear to a request for a lock of his hair to patch a favorite doormat with, resumed with much vigor his task of sweeping up the litter.

The most dressy sailorman I ever knew, he continued, as he stood the broom up in a corner and seated himself on a keg, was a young feller named Rupert Brown. His mother gave 'im the name of Rupert while his father was away at sea, and when he came 'ome it was too late to alter it. All that a man could do he did do, and Mrs. Brown 'ad a black eye till 'e went to sea agin. She was a very obstinate woman, though—like most of 'em—and a little over a year arterwards got pore old Brown three months' hard by naming 'er next boy Roderick Alfonso.

Young Rupert was on a barge when I knew 'im fust, but he got tired of always 'aving dirty hands arter a time, and went and enlisted as a soldier. I lost sight of 'im for a while, and then one evening he turned up on furlough and come to see me.

O' course, by this time 'e was tired of soldiering, but wot upset 'im more than anything was always 'aving to be dressed the same and not being able to wear a collar and neck-tie. He said that if it wasn't for the sake of good old England, and the chance o' getting six months, he'd desert. I tried to give 'im good advice, and, if I'd only known 'ow I was to be dragged into it, I'd ha' given 'im a lot more.

As it 'appened he deserted the very next arternoon. He was in the Three Widders at Aldgate, in the saloon bar—which is a place where you get a penn'orth of ale in a glass and pay twopence for it—

and, arter being told by the barmaid that she had got one monkey at 'ome, he got into conversation with another man wot was in there.

He was a big man with a black moustache and a red face, and 'is fingers all smothered in di'mond rings. He 'ad got on a gold watch-chain as thick as a rope, and a scarf-pin the size of a large walnut, and he had 'ad a few words with the barmaid on 'is own account. He seemed to take a fancy to Rupert from the fust, and in a few minutes he 'ad given 'im a big cigar out of a sealskin case and ordered 'im a glass of sherry wine.

"Have you ever thought o' going on the stage?" he ses, arter Rupert 'ad told 'im of his dislike for the Army.

"No," ses Rupert, staring.

"You s'prise me," ses the big man; "you're wasting of your life by not doing so."

"But I can't act," ses Rupert.

"Stuff and nonsense!" ses the big man. "Don't tell me. You've got an actor's face. I'm a manager myself, and I know. I don't mind telling you that I refused twenty-three men and forty-eight ladies only yesterday."

"I wonder you don't drop down dead," ses the barmaid, lifting up 'is glass to wipe down the counter.

The manager looked at her, and, arter she 'ad gone to talk to a gentleman in the next bar wot was knocking double knocks on the counter with a pint pot, he whispered to Rupert that she 'ad been one of them.

"She can't act a bit," he ses. "Now, look 'ere; I'm a business man and my time is valuable. I don't know nothing, and I don't want to know nothing; but, if a nice young feller, like yourself, for example, was tired of the Army and wanted to escape, I've got one part left in my company that 'ud suit 'im down to the ground."

"Wot about being reckernized?" ses Rupert.

The manager winked at 'im. "It's the part of a Zulu chief," he ses, in a whisper.

Rupert started. "But I should 'ave to black my face," he ses.

"A little," ses the manager; "but you'd soon get on to better parts—and see wot a fine disguise it is."

He stood 'im two more glasses o' sherry wine, and, arter he' ad drunk 'em, Rupert gave way. The manager patted 'im on the back, and said that if he wasn't earning fifty pounds a week in a year's time he'd eat his 'ead; and the barmaid, wot 'ad come back agin, said it was the best thing he could do with it, and she wondered he 'adn't thought of it afore.

They went out separate, as the manager said it would be better for them not to be seen together, and Rupert, keeping about a dozen yards behind, follered 'im down the Mile End Road. By and by the manager stopped outside a shop-window wot 'ad been boarded up and stuck all over with savages dancing and killing white people and hunting elephants, and, arter turning round and giving Rupert a nod, opened the door with a key and went inside.

"That's all right," he ses, as Rupert follered 'im in. "This is my wife, Mrs. Alfredi," he ses, introducing 'im to a fat, red-'aired lady wot was sitting inside sewing. "She has performed before all the crowned 'eads of Europe. That di'mond brooch she's wearing was a present from the Emperor of Germany, but, being a married man, he asked 'er to keep it quiet."

Rupert shook 'ands with Mrs. Alfredi, and then her 'usband led 'im to a room at the back, where a little lame man was cleaning up things, and told 'im to take his clothes off.

"If they was mine," he ses, squinting at the fire-place, "I should know wot to do with 'em."

Rupert laughed and slapped 'im on the back, and, arter cutting his uniform into pieces, stuffed it into the fireplace and pulled the dampers out. He burnt up 'is boots and socks and everything else, and they all three laughed as though it was the best joke in the world. Then Mr. Alfredi took his coat off and, dipping a piece of rag into a basin of stuff wot George 'ad fetched, did Rupert a lovely brown all over.

"That's the fust coat," he ses. "Now take a stool in front of the fire and let it soak in."

He gave 'im another coat arf an hour arterwards, while George curled his 'air, and when 'e was dressed in bracelets round 'is ankles and wrists, and a leopard-skin over his shoulder, he was as fine a Zulu as you could wish for to see. His lips was naturally thick and his nose flat, and even his eyes 'appened to be about the right color.

"He's a fair perfect treat," ses Mr. Alfredi. "Fetch Kumbo in, George."

The little man went out, and came back agin shoving in a fat, stumpy Zulu woman wot began to grin and chatter like a poll-parrot the moment she saw Rupert.

"It's all right," ses Mr. Alfredi; "she's took a fancy to you."

"Is—is she an actress?" ses Rupert.

"One o' the best," ses the manager. "She'll teach you to dance and shy assegais. Pore thing! she buried her 'usband the day afore we come here, but you'll be surprised to see 'ow skittish she can be when she has got over it a bit."

They sat there while Rupert practised—till he started shying the assegais, that is—and then they went out and left 'im with Kumbo. Considering that she 'ad only just buried her 'usband, Rupert found her quite skittish enough, and he couldn't 'elp wondering wot she'd be like when she'd got over her grief a bit more.

The manager and George said he 'ad got on wonderfully, and arter talking it over with Mrs. Alfredi they decided to open that evening, and pore Rupert found out that the shop was the theatre, and all the acting he'd got to do was to dance war-dances and sing in Zulu to people wot had paid a penny a 'ead. He was a bit nervous at fust, for fear anybody should find out that 'e wasn't a real Zulu, because the manager said they'd tear 'im to pieces if they did, and eat 'im arterwards, but arter a time 'is nervousness wore off and he jumped about like a monkey.

They gave performances every arf hour from ha'-past six to ten, and Rupert felt ready to drop. His feet was sore with dancing and his throat ached with singing Zulu, but wot upset 'im more than anything was an elderly old party wot would keep jabbing 'im in the ribs with her umbrella to see whether he could laugh.

They 'ad supper arter they 'ad closed, and then Mr. Alfredi and 'is wife went off, and Rupert and George made up beds for themselves in the shop, while Kumbo 'ad a little place to herself at the back.

He did better than ever next night, and they all said he was improving fast; and Mr. Alfredi told 'im in a whisper that he thought he was better at it than Kumbo. "Not that I should mind 'er knowing much," he ses, "seeing that she's took such a fancy to you."

"Ah, I was going to speak to you about that," ses Rupert. "Forwardness is no name for it; if she don't keep 'erself to 'erself, I shall chuck the whole thing up."

The manager coughed behind his 'and. "And go back to the Army?" he ses. "Well, I should be sorry to lose you, but I won't stand in your way."

Mrs. Alfredi, wot was standing by, stuffed her pocket-'ankercher in 'er mouth, and Rupert began to feel a bit uneasy in his mind.

"If I did," he ses, "you'd get into trouble for 'elping me to desert."

"Desert!" ses Mr. Alfredi. "I don't know anything about your deserting."

"Ho!" ses Rupert. "And wot about my uniform?"

"Uniform?" ses Mr. Alfredi. "Wot uniform? I ain't seen no uniform. Where is it?"

Rupert didn't answer 'im, but arter they 'ad gone 'ome he told George that he 'ad 'ad enough of acting and he should go.

"Where to?" ses George.

"I'll find somewhere," ses Rupert. "I sha'n't starve."

"You might ketch your death o' cold, though," ses George.

Rupert said he didn't mind, and then he shut 'is eyes and pretended to be asleep. His idea was to wait till George was asleep and then pinch 'is clothes; consequently 'is feelings when 'e opened one eye and saw George getting into bed with 'is clothes on won't bear thinking about. He laid awake for hours, and three times that night George, who was a very heavy sleeper, woke up and found Rupert busy tucking him in.

By the end of the week Rupert was getting desperate. He hated being black for one thing, and the more he washed the better color he looked. He didn't mind the black for out o' doors, in case the Army was looking for 'im, but 'aving no clothes he couldn't get out o' doors; and when he said he wouldn't perform unless he got some, Mr. Alfredi dropped 'ints about having 'im took up for a deserter.

"I've 'ad my suspicions of it for some days," he ses, with a wink, "though you did come to me in a nice serge suit and tell me you was an actor. Now, you be a good boy for another week and I'll advance you a couple o' pounds to get some clothes with."

Rupert asked him to let 'im have it then, but 'e wouldn't, and for another week he 'ad to pretend 'e was a Zulu of an evening, and try and persuade Kumbo that he was an English gentleman of a daytime.

He got the money at the end of the week and 'ad to sign a paper to give a month's notice any time he wanted to leave, but he didn't mind that at all, being determined the fust time he got outside the place to run away and ship as a nigger cook if 'e couldn't get the black off.

He made a list o' things out for George to get for 'im, but there seemed to be such a lot for two pounds that Mr. Alfredi shook his 'ead over it; and arter calling 'imself a soft-'arted fool, and saying he'd finish up in the workhouse, he made it three pounds and told George to look sharp.

"He's a very good marketer," he ses, arter George 'ad gone; "he don't mind wot trouble he takes. He'll very likely haggle for hours to get sixpence knocked off the trousers or twopence off the shirt."

It was twelve o'clock in the morning when George went, and at ha'-past four Rupert turned nasty, and said 'e was afraid he was trying to get them for nothing. At five o'clock he said George was a fool, and at ha'-past he said 'e was something I won't repeat.

It was just eleven o'clock, and they 'ad shut up for the night, when the front door opened, and George stood there smiling at 'em and shaking his 'ead.

"Sush a lark," he ses, catching 'old of Mr. Alfredi's arm to steady 'imself. "I gave 'im shlip."

"Wot d'ye mean?" ses the manager, shaking him off. "Gave who the slip? Where's them clothes?"

"Boy's got 'em," ses George, smiling agin and catching hold of Kumbo's arm. "Sush a lark; he's been car-carrying 'em all day—all day. Now I've given 'im the—the shlip, 'stead o'—'stead o' giving 'im fourpence. Take care o' the pensh, an' pouns—"

He let go o' Kumbo's arm, turned round twice, and then sat down 'eavy and fell fast asleep. The manager rushed to the door and looked out, but there was no signs of the boy, and he came back shaking his 'ead, and said that George 'ad been drinking again.

"Well, wot about my clothes?" ses Rupert, hardly able to speak.

"P'r'aps he didn't buy 'em arter all," ses the manager. "Let's try 'is pockets."

He tried fust, and found some strawberries that George 'ad spoilt by sitting on. Then he told Rupert to have a try, and Rupert found some bits of string, a few buttons, two penny stamps, and twopence ha'penny in coppers.

"Never mind," ses Mr. Alfredi; "I'll go round to the police-station in the morning; p'r'aps the boy 'as taken them there. I'm disapp'inted in George. I shall tell 'im so, too."

He bid Rupert good-night and went off with Mrs. Alfredi; and Rupert, wishful to make the best o' things, decided that he would undress George and go off in 'is clothes. He waited till Kumbo 'ad gone off to bed, and then he started to take George's coat off. He got the two top buttons undone all right, and then George turned over in 'is sleep. It surprised Rupert, but wot surprised 'im more when he rolled George over was to find them two buttons done up agin. Arter it had 'appened three times he see 'ow it was, and he come to the belief that George was no more drunk than wot he was, and that it was all a put-up thing between 'im and Mr. Alfredi.

He went to bed then to think it over, and by the morning he 'ad made up his mind to keep quiet and bide his time, as the saying is. He spoke quite cheerful to Mr. Alfredi, and pretended to believe 'im when he said that he 'ad been to the police-station about the clothes.

Two days arterwards he thought of something; he remembered me. He 'ad found a dirty old envelope on the floor, and with a bit o' lead pencil he wrote me a letter on the back of one o' the bills, telling me all his troubles, and asking me to bring some clothes and rescue 'im. He stuck on one of the stamps he 'ad found in George's pocket, and opening the door just afore going to bed threw it out on the pavement.

The world is full of officious, interfering busy-bodies. I should no more think of posting a letter that didn't belong to me, with an unused stamp on it, than I should think o' flying; but some meddle-some son of a—a gun posted that letter and I got it.

I was never more surprised in my life. He asked me to be outside the shop next night at ha'-past eleven with any old clothes I could pick up. If I didn't, he said he should 'ang 'imself as the clock struck twelve, and that his ghost would sit on the wharf and keep watch with me every night for the rest o' my life. He said he expected it 'ud have a black face, same as in life.

A wharf is a lonely place of a night; especially our wharf, which is full of dark corners, and, being a silly, good-natured fool, I went. I got a pal off of one of the boats to keep watch for me, and, arter getting some old rags off of another sailorman as owed me arf a dollar, I 'ad a drink and started off for the Mile End Road.

I found the place easy enough. The door was just on the jar, and as I tapped on it with my finger-nails a wild-looking black man, arf naked, opened it and said "H'sh!" and pulled me inside. There was a bit o' candle on the floor, shaded by a box, and a man fast asleep and snoring up in one corner. Rupert dressed like lightning, and he 'ad just put on 'is cap when the door at the back opened and a 'orrid fat black woman came out and began to chatter.

Rupert told her to hush, and she 'ushed, and then he waved 'is hand to 'er to say "good-bye," and afore you could say Jack Robinson she 'ad grabbed up a bit o' dirty blanket, a bundle of assegais, and a spear, and come out arter us.

"Back!" ses Rupert in a whisper, pointing.

Kumbo shook her 'ead, and then he took hold of 'er and tried to shove 'er back, but she wouldn't go. I lent him a 'and, but all wimmen are the same, black or white, and afore I knew where I was she 'ad clawed my cap off and scratched me all down one side of the face.

"Walk fast," ses Rupert.

I started to run, but it was all no good; Kumbo kept up with us easy, and she was so pleased at being out in the open air that she began to dance and play about like a kitten. Instead o' minding their own business people turned and follered us, and quite a crowd collected.

"We shall 'ave the police in a minute," ses Rupert. "Come in 'ere— quick."

He pointed to a pub up a side street, and went in with Kumbo holding on to his arm. The barman was for sending us out at fust, but such a crowd follered us in that he altered 'is mind. I ordered three pints, and, while I was 'anding Rupert his, Kumbo finished 'ers and began on mine. I tried to explain, but she held on to it like grim death, and in the confusion Rupert slipped out.

He 'adn't been gone five seconds afore she missed 'im, and I never see anybody so upset in all my life. She spilt the beer all down the place where 'er bodice ought to ha' been, and then she dropped the pot and went arter 'im like a hare. I follered in a different way, and when I got round the corner I found she 'ad caught 'im and was holding 'im by the arm.

O' course, the crowd was round us agin, and to get rid of 'em I did a thing I'd seldom done afore—I called a cab, and we all bundled in and drove off to the wharf, with the spear sticking out o' the window, and most of the assegais sticking into me.

"This is getting serious," ses Rupert.

"Yes," I ses; "and wot 'ave I done to be dragged into it? You must ha' been paying 'er some attention to make 'er carry on like this."

I thought Rupert would ha' bust, and the things he said to the man wot was spending money like water to rescue 'im was disgraceful.

We got to the wharf at last, and I was glad to see that my pal 'ad got tired of night-watching and 'ad gone off, leaving the gate open. Kumbo went in 'anging on to Rupert's arm, and I follered with the spear, which I 'ad held in my 'and while I paid the cabman.

They went into the office, and Rupert and me talked it over while Kumbo kept patting 'is cheek. He was afraid that the manager would track 'im to the wharf, and I was afraid that the guv'nor would find out that I 'ad been neglecting my dooty, for the fust time in my life.

We talked all night pretty near, and then, at ha'-past five, arf an hour afore the 'ands came on, I made up my mind to fetch a cab and drive 'em to my 'ouse. I wanted Rupert to go somewhere else, but 'e said he 'ad got nowhere else to go, and it was the only thing to get 'em off the wharf. I opened the gates at ten minutes to six, and just as the fust man come on and walked down the wharf we slipped in and drove away.

We was all tired and yawning. There's something about the motion of a cab or an omnibus that always makes me feel sleepy, and arter a time I closed my eyes and went off sound. I remember I was dreaming that I 'ad found a bag o' money, when the cab pulled up with a jerk in front of my 'ouse and woke me up. Opposite me sat Kumbo fast asleep, and Rupert 'ad disappeared!

I was dazed for a moment, and afore I could do anything Kumbo woke up and missed Rupert. Wot made matters worse than anything was that my missis was kneeling down in the passage doing 'er door-step, and 'er face, as I got down out o' that cab with Kumbo 'anging on to my arm was something too awful for words. It seemed to rise up slow-like from near the door-step, and to go on rising till I thought it 'ud never stop. And every inch it rose it got worse and worse to look at.

She stood blocking up the doorway with her 'ands on her 'ips, while I explained, with Kumbo still 'anging on my arm and a crowd collecting behind, and the more I explained, the more I could see she didn't believe a word of it.

She never 'as believed it. I sent for Mr. Alfredi to come and take Kumbo away, and when I spoke to 'im about Rupert he said I was dreaming, and asked me whether I wasn't ashamed o' myself for carrying off a pore black gal wot 'ad got no father or mother to look arter her. He said that afore my missis, and my character 'as been under a cloud ever since, waiting for Rupert to turn up and clear it away.

DIRTY WORK

It was nearly high-water, and the night-watchman, who had stepped aboard a lighter lying alongside the wharf to smoke a pipe, sat with half-closed eyes enjoying the summer evening. The bustle of the day was over, the wharves were deserted, and hardly a craft moved on the river. Perfumed clouds of shag, hovering for a time over the lighter, floated lazily towards the Surrey shore.

"There's one thing about my job," said the night-watchman, slowly, "it's done all alone by yourself. There's no foreman a-hollering at you and offering you a penny for your thoughts, and no mates to run into you from behind with a loaded truck and then ask you why you didn't look where you're going to. From six o'clock in the evening to six o'clock next morning I'm my own master."

He rammed down the tobacco with an experienced forefinger and puffed contentedly.

People like you 'ud find it lonely (he continued, after a pause); I did at fust. I used to let people come and sit 'ere with me of an evening talking, but I got tired of it arter a time, and when one chap fell overboard while 'e was showing me 'ow he put his wife's mother in 'er place, I gave it up altogether. There was three foot o' mud in the dock at the time, and arter I 'ad got 'im out, he fainted in my arms.

Arter that I kept myself to myself. Say wot you like, a man's best friend is 'imself. There's nobody else'll do as much for 'im, or let 'im off easier when he makes a mistake. If I felt a bit lonely I used to open the wicket in the gate and sit there watching the road, and p'r'aps pass a word or two with the policeman. Then something 'appened one night that made me take quite a dislike to it for a time.

I was sitting there with my feet outside, smoking a quiet pipe, when I 'eard a bit of a noise in the distance. Then I 'eard people running and shouts of "Stop, thief!" A man came along round the corner full pelt, and, just as I got up, dashed through the wicket and ran on to the wharf. I was arter 'im like a shot and got up to 'im just in time to see him throw something into the dock. And at the same moment I 'eard the other people run past the gate.

"Wot's up?" I ses, collaring 'im.

"Nothing," he ses, breathing 'ard and struggling. "Let me go."

He was a little wisp of a man, and I shook 'im like a dog shakes a rat. I remembered my own pocket being picked, and I nearly shook the breath out of 'im.

"And now I'm going to give you in charge," I ses, pushing 'im along towards the gate.

"Wot for?" he ses, purtending to be surprised.

"Stealing," I ses.

"You've made a mistake," he ses; "you can search me if you like."

"More use to search the dock," I ses. "I see you throw it in. Now you keep quiet, else you'll get 'urt. If you get five years I shall be all the more pleased."

I don't know 'ow he did it, but 'e did. He seemed to sink away between my legs, and afore I knew wot was 'appening, I was standing upside down with all the blood rushing to my 'ead. As I rolled over he bolted through the wicket, and was off like a flash of lightning.

A couple o' minutes arterwards the people wot I 'ad 'eard run past came back agin. There was a big fat policeman with 'em—a man I'd seen afore on the beat—and, when they 'ad gorn on, he stopped to 'ave a word with me.

"'Ot work," he ses, taking off his 'elmet and wiping his bald 'ead with a large red handkerchief. "I've lost all my puff."

"Been running?" I ses, very perlite.

"Arter a pickpocket," he ses. "He snatched a lady's purse just as she was stepping aboard the French boat with her 'usband. 'Twelve pounds in it in gold, two peppermint lozenges, and a postage stamp.'"

He shook his 'ead, and put his 'elmet on agin.

"Holding it in her little 'and as usual," he ses. "Asking for trouble, I call it. I believe if a woman 'ad one hand off and only a finger and thumb left on the other, she'd carry 'er purse in it."

He knew a'most as much about wimmen as I do. When 'is fust wife died, she said 'er only wish was that she could take 'im with her, and she made 'im promise her faithful that 'e'd never marry agin. His second wife, arter a long illness, passed away while he was playing hymns on the concertina to her, and 'er mother, arter looking at 'er very hard, went to the doctor and said she wanted an inquest.

He went on talking for a long time, but I was busy doing a bit of 'ead-work and didn't pay much attention to 'im. I was thinking o' twelve pounds, two lozenges, and a postage stamp laying in the mud at the bottom of my dock, and arter a time 'e said 'e see as 'ow I was waiting to get back to my night's rest, and went off—stamping.

I locked the wicket when he 'ad gorn away, and then I went to the edge of the dock and stood looking down at the spot where the purse 'ad been chucked in. The tide was on the ebb, but there was still a foot or two of water atop of the mud. I walked up and down, thinking.

I thought for a long time, and then I made up my mind. If I got the purse and took it to the police-station the police would share the money out between 'em, and tell me they 'ad given it back to the lady. If I found it and put a notice in the newspaper—which would cost money—very likely a dozen or two ladies would come and see me and say it was theirs. Then if I gave it to the best-looking one and the one it belonged to turned up, there'd be trouble. My idea was to keep it—for a time—and then if the lady who lost it came to me and asked me for it I would give it to 'er.

Once I had made up my mind to do wot was right I felt quite 'appy, and arter a look up and down, I stepped round to the Bear's Head and 'ad a couple o' goes o' rum to keep the cold out. There was nobody in there but the landlord, and 'e started at once talking about the thief, and 'ow he 'ad run arter him in 'is shirt-sleeves.

"My opinion is," he ses, "that 'e bolted on one of the wharves and 'id 'imself. He disappeared like magic. Was that little gate o' yours open?"

"I was on the wharf," I ses, very cold.

"You might ha' been on the wharf and yet not 'ave seen anybody come on," he ses, nodding.

"Wot d'ye mean?" I ses, very sharp. "Nothing," he ses. "Nothing."

"Are you trying to take my character away?" I ses, fixing 'im with my eye.

"Lo' bless me, no!" he ses, staring at me. "It's no good to me."

He sat down in 'is chair behind the bar and went straight off to sleep with his eyes screwed up as tight as they would go. Then 'e opened his mouth and snored till the glasses shook. I suppose I've been one of the best customers he ever 'ad, and that's the way he treated me. For two pins I'd ha' knocked 'is ugly 'ead off, but arter waking him up very sudden by dropping my glass on the floor I went off back to the wharf.

I locked up agin, and 'ad another look at the dock. The water 'ad nearly gone and the mud was showing in patches. My mind went back to a sailorman wot had dropped 'is watch over-board two years before, and found it by walking about in the dock in 'is bare feet. He found it more easy because the glass broke when he trod on it.

The evening was a trifle chilly for June, but I've been used to roughing it all my life, especially when I was afloat, and I went into the office and began to take my clothes off. I took off everything but my pants, and I made sure o' them by making braces for 'em out of a bit of string. Then I turned the gas low, and, arter slipping on my boots, went outside.

It was so cold that at fust I thought I'd give up the idea. The longer I stood on the edge looking at the mud the colder it looked, but at last I turned round and went slowly down the ladder. I waited a moment at the bottom, and was just going to step off when I remembered that I 'ad got my boots on, and I 'ad to go up agin and take 'em off.

I went down very slow the next time, and anybody who 'as been down an iron ladder with thin, cold rungs, in their bare feet, will know why, and I had just dipped my left foot in, when the wharf-bell rang.

I 'oped at fust that it was a runaway-ring, but it kept on, and the longer it kept on, the worse it got. I went up that ladder agin and called out that I was coming, and then I went into the office and just slipped on my coat and trousers and went to the gate.

"Wot d'you want?" I ses, opening the wicket three or four inches and looking out at a man wot was standing there.

"Are you old Bill?" he ses.

"I'm the watchman," I ses, sharp-like. "Wot d'you want?"

"Don't bite me!" he ses, purtending to draw back. "I ain't done no 'arm. I've come round about that glass you smashed at the Bear's Head."

"Glass!" I ses, 'ardly able to speak.

"Yes, glass," he ses—"thing wot yer drink out of. The landlord says it'll cost you a tanner, and 'e wants it now in case you pass away in your sleep. He couldn't come 'imself cos he's got nobody to mind the bar, so 'e sent me. Why! Halloa! Where's your boots? Ain't you afraid o' ketching cold?"

"You clear off," I ses, shouting at him. "D'ye 'ear me? Clear off while you're safe, and you tell the landlord that next time 'e insults me I'll smash every glass in 'is place and then sit 'im on top of 'em! Tell 'im if 'e wants a tanner out o' me, to come round 'imself, and see wot he gets."

It was a silly thing to say, and I saw it arterwards, but I was in such a temper I 'ardly knew wot I was saying. I slammed the wicket in 'is face and turned the key and then I took off my clothes and went down that ladder agin.

It seemed colder than ever, and the mud when I got fairly into it was worse than I thought it could ha' been. It stuck to me like glue, and every step I took seemed colder than the one before. 'Owever, when I make up my mind to do a thing, I do it. I fixed my eyes on the place where I thought the purse was, and every time I felt anything under my foot I reached down and picked it up—and then chucked it away as far as I could so as not to pick it up agin. Dirty job it was, too, and in five minutes I was mud up to the neck, a'most. And I 'ad just got to wot I thought was the right place, and feeling about very careful, when the bell rang agin.

I thought I should ha' gorn out o' my mind. It was just a little tinkle at first, then another tinkle, but, as I stood there all in the dark and cold trying to make up my mind to take no notice of it, it began to ring like mad. I 'ad to go—I've known men climb over the gate afore now—and I didn't want to be caught in that dock.

The mud seemed stickier than ever, but I got out at last, and, arter scraping some of it off with a bit o' stick. I put on my coat and trousers and boots just as I was and went to the gate, with the bell going its 'ardest all the time.

When I opened the gate and see the landlord of the Bear's Head standing there I turned quite dizzy, and there was a noise in my ears like the roaring of the sea. I should think I stood there for a couple o' minutes without being able to say a word. I could think of 'em.

"Don't be frightened, Bill," ses the landlord. "I'm not going to eat you."

"He looks as if he's walking in 'is sleep," ses the fat policeman, wot was standing near by. "Don't startle 'im."

"He always looks like that," ses the landlord.

I stood looking at 'im. I could speak then, but I couldn't think of any words good enough; not with a policeman standing by with a notebook in 'is pocket.

"Wot was you ringing my bell for?" I ses, at last.

"Why didn't you answer it before?" ses the landlord. "D'you think I've got nothing better to do than to stand ringing your bell for three-quarters of an hour? Some people would report you."

"I know my dooty," I ses; "there's no craft up to-night, and no reason for anybody to come to my bell. If I was to open the gate every time a parcel of overgrown boys rang my bell I should 'ave enough to do."

"Well, I'll overlook it this time, seeing as you're an old man and couldn't get another sleeping-in job," he ses, looking at the policeman for him to see 'ow clever 'e was. "Wot about that tanner? That's wot I've come for."

"You be off," I ses, starting to shut the wicket. "You won't get no tanner out of me."

"All right," he ses, "I shall stand here and go on ringing the bell till you pay up, that's all."

He gave it another tug, and the policeman instead of locking 'im up for it stood there laughing.

I gave 'im the tanner. It was no use standing there arguing over a tanner, with a purse of twelve quid waiting for me in the dock, but I told 'im wot people thought of 'im.

"Arf a second, watchman," ses the policeman, as I started to shut the wicket agin. "You didn't see anything of that pickpocket, did you?"

"I did not," I ses.

"'Cos this gentleman thought he might 'ave come in here," ses the policeman.

"'Ow could he 'ave come in here without me knowing it?" I ses, firing up.

"Easy," ses the landlord, "and stole your boots into the bargain"

"He might 'ave come when your back was turned," ses the policeman, "and if so, he might be 'iding there now. I wonder whether you'd mind me having a look round?"

"I tell you he ain't 'ere," I ses, very short, "but, to ease your mind, I'll 'ave a look round myself arter you've gorn."

The policeman shook his 'ead. "Well, o' course, I can't come in without your permission," he ses, with a little cough, "but I 'ave an idea, that if it was your guv'nor 'ere instead of you he'd ha' been on'y too pleased to do anything 'e could to help the law. I'll beg his pardon tomorrow for asking you, in case he might object."

That settled it. That's the police all over, and that's 'ow they get their way and do as they like. I could see 'im in my mind's eye talking to the guv'nor, and letting out little things about broken glasses and such-like by accident. I drew back to let 'im pass, and I was so upset that when that little rat of a landlord follered 'im I didn't say a word.

I stood and watched them poking and prying about the wharf as if it belonged to 'em, with the light from the policeman's lantern flashing about all over the place. I was shivering with cold and temper. The mud was drying on me.

"If you've finished 'unting for the pickpocket I'll let you out and get on with my work," I ses, drawing myself up.

"Good night," ses the policeman, moving off. "Good night, dear," ses the landlord. "Mind you tuck yourself up warm."

I lost my temper for the moment and afore I knew wot I was doing I 'ad got hold of him and was shoving 'im towards the gate as 'ard as I could shove. He pretty near got my coat off in the struggle, and next moment the police-man 'ad turned his lantern on me and they was both staring at me as if they couldn't believe their eyesight.

"He—he's turning black!" ses the landlord.

"He's turned black!" ses the policeman.

They both stood there looking at me with their mouths open, and then afore I knew wot he was up to, the policeman came close up to me and scratched my chest with his finger-nail.

"It's mud " he ses.

"You keep your nails to yourself," I ses. "It's nothing to do with you." and I couldn't 'elp noticing the smell of it. Nobody could. And wot was worse than all was, that the tide 'ad turned and was creeping over the mud in the dock.

They got tired of it at last and came back to where I was and stood there shaking their 'eads at me.

"If he was on the wharf 'e must 'ave made his escape while you was in the Bear's Head," ses the policeman.

"He was in my place a long time," ses the landlord.

"Well, it's no use crying over spilt milk," ses the policeman. "Funny smell about 'ere, ain't there?" he ses, sniffing, and turning to the landlord. "Wot is it?"

"I dunno," ses the landlord. "I noticed it while we was talking to 'im at the gate. It seems to foller 'im about."

"I've smelt things I like better," ses the policeman, sniffing agin. "It's just like the foreshore when somebody 'as been stirring the mud up a bit."

"Unless it's a case of 'tempted suicide," he ses, looking at me very 'ard.

"Ah!" ses the landlord.

"There's no mud on 'is clothes," ses the policeman, looking me over with his lantern agin.

"He must 'ave gone in naked, but I should like to see 'is legs to make— All right! All right! Keep your 'air on."

"You look arter your own legs, then," I ses, very sharp, "and mind your own business."

"It is my business," he ses, turning to the landlord. "Was 'e strange in his manner at all when 'e was in your place to-night?"

"He smashed one o' my best glasses," ses the landlord.

"So he did," ses the policeman. "So he did. I'd forgot that. Do you know 'im well?"

"Not more than I can 'elp," ses the landlord. "He's been in my place a good bit, but I never knew of any reason why 'e should try and do away with 'imself. If he's been disappointed in love, he ain't told me anything about it."

I suppose that couple o' fools 'ud 'ave stood there talking about me all night if I'd ha' let 'em, but I had about enough of it.

"Look 'ere," I ses, "you're very clever, both of you, but you needn't worry your 'eads about me. I've just been having a mud-bath, that's all."

"A mud-bath!" ses both of 'em, squeaking like a couple o' silly parrots.

"For rheumatics," I ses. "I 'ad it some-thing cruel to-night, and I thought that p'r'aps the mud 'ud do it good. I read about it in the papers. There's places where you pay pounds and pounds for 'em, but, being a pore man, I 'ad to 'ave mine on the cheap."

The policeman stood there looking at me for a moment, and then 'e began to laugh till he couldn't stop 'imself.

"Love-a-duck!" he ses, at last, wiping his eyes. "I wish I'd seen it."

"Must ha' looked like a fat mermaid," ses the landlord, wagging his silly 'ead at me. "I can just see old Bill sitting in the mud a-combing his 'air and singing."

They 'ad some more talk o' that sort, just to show each other 'ow funny they was, but they went off at last, and I fastened up the gate and went into the office to clean myself up as well as I could. One comfort was they 'adn't got the least idea of wot I was arter, and I 'ad a fancy that the one as laughed last would be the one as got that twelve quid.

I was so tired that I slept nearly all day arter I 'ad got 'ome, and I 'ad no sooner got back to the wharf in the evening than I see that the landlord 'ad been busy. If there was one silly fool that asked me the best way of making mud-pies, I should think there was fifty. Little things please little minds, and the silly way some of 'em went on made me feel sorry for my sects.

By eight o'clock, 'owever, they 'ad all sheered off, and I got a broom and began to sweep up to 'elp pass the time away until low-water. On'y one craft 'ad come up that day—a ketch called the Peewit—and as she was berthed at the end of the jetty she wasn't in my way at all.

Her skipper came on to the wharf just afore ten. Fat, silly old man 'e was, named Fogg. Always talking about 'is 'ealth and taking medicine to do it good. He came up to me slow like, and, when 'e stopped and asked me about the rheumatics, the broom shook in my 'and.

"Look here," I ses, "if you want to be funny, go and be funny with them as likes it. I'm fair sick of it, so I give you warning."

"Funny?" he ses, staring at me with eyes like a cow. "Wot d'ye mean? There's nothing funny about rheumatics; I ought to know; I'm a martyr to it. Did you find as 'ow the mud did you any good?"

I looked at 'im hard, but 'e stood there looking at me with his fat baby-face, and I knew he didn't mean any harm; so I answered 'im perlite and wished 'im good night.

"I've 'ad pretty near everything a man can have," he ses, casting anchor on a empty box, "but I think the rheumatics was about the worst of 'em all. I even tried bees for it once."

"Bees!" I ses. "*Bees!*"

"Bee-stings," he ses. "A man told me that if I could on'y persuade a few bees to sting me, that 'ud cure me. I don't know what 'e meant by persuading! they didn't want no persuading. I took off my coat and shirt and went and rocked one of my neighbour's bee-hives next door, and I thought my last hour 'ad come."

He sat on that box and shivered at the memory of it.

"Now I take Dr. Pepper's pellets instead," he ses. "I've got a box in my state-room, and if you'd like to try 'em you're welcome."

He sat there talking about the complaints he had 'ad and wot he 'ad done for them till I thought I should never have got rid of 'im. He got up at last, though, and, arter telling me to always wear flannel next to my skin, climbed aboard and went below.

I knew the hands was aboard, and arter watching 'is cabin-skylight until the light was out, I went and undressed. Then I crept back on to the jetty, and arter listening by the Peewit to make sure that they was all asleep, I went back and climbed down the ladder.

It was colder than ever. The cold seemed to get into my bones, but I made up my mind to 'ave that twelve quid if I died for it. I trod round and round the place where I 'ad seen that purse chucked in until I was tired, and the rubbish I picked up by mistake you wouldn't believe.

I suppose I 'ad been in there arf an hour, and I was standing up with my teeth clenched to keep them from chattering, when I 'appened to look round and see something like a white ball coming down the ladder. My 'art seemed to stand still for a moment, and then it began to beat as though it would burst. The white thing came down lower and lower, and then all of a sudden it stood in the mud and said, "Ow!"

"Who is it?" I ses. "Who are you?" "Halloa, Bill!" it ses. "Ain't it perishing cold?"

It was the voice o' Cap'n Fogg, and if ever I wanted to kill a fellow-creetur, I wanted to then.

"'Ave you been in long, Bill?" he ses. "About ten minutes," I ses, grinding my teeth.

"Is it doing you good?" he ses.

I didn't answer 'im.

"I was just going off to sleep," he ses, "when I felt a sort of hot pain in my left knee. O' course, I knew what it meant at once, and instead o' taking some of the pellets I thought I'd try your remedy instead. It's a bit nippy, but I don't mind that if it does me good."

He laughed a silly sort o' laugh, and then I'm blest if 'e didn't sit down in that mud and waller in it. Then he'd get up and come for'ard two or three steps and sit down agin.

"Ain't you sitting down, Bill?" he ses, arter a time.

"No," I ses, "I'm not."

"I don't think you can expect to get the full benefit unless you do," he ses, coming up close to me and sitting down agin. "It's a bit of a shock at fust, but Halloa!"

"Wot's up?" I ses.

"Sitting on something hard," he ses. "I wish people 'ud be more careful."

He took a list to port and felt under the star-board side. Then he brought his 'and up and tried to wipe the mud off and see wot he 'ad got.

"Wot is it?" I ses, with a nasty sinking sort o' feeling inside me.

"I don't know," he ses, going on wiping. "It's soft outside and 'ard inside. It—"

"Let's 'ave a look at it," I ses, holding out my 'and.

"It's nothing," he ses, in a queer voice, getting up and steering for the ladder. "Bit of oyster-shell, I think."

He was up that ladder hand over fist, with me close behind 'im, and as soon as he 'ad got on to the wharf started to run to 'is ship.

"Good night, Bill," he ses, over 'is shoulder.

"Arf a moment." I ses, follering 'im.

"I must get aboard," he ses; "I believe I've got a chill," and afore I could stop 'im he 'ad jumped on and run down to 'is cabin.

I stood on the jetty for a minute or two, trembling all over with cold and temper. Then I saw he 'ad got a light in 'is cabin, and I crept aboard and peeped down the skylight. And I just 'ad time to see some sovereigns on the table, when he looked up and blew out the light.

William Wymark Jacobs was born on September 8, 1863 in the Wapping district of London, England. An author, humorist and dramatist, Jacobs is best remembered for the enduring classic tale of horror - "The Monkey's Paw".

As a youth, Jacobs grew up near the Wapping docks in London, where his father was a wharf manager. The family's first home was home was a house on a River Thames wharf.

The docklands setting would show up frequently in his later literary output. Jacobs, the wharf rat, and his three siblings lost their mother when they were all still young children. Their father, William Gage Jacobs, remarried and fathered a further seven children with his erstwhile housekeeper Ellen Florey. Although he grew up surrounded by poverty, Jacobs himself received a formal education in London, first at a private prep school and later at the Birkbeck Literary and Scientific Institute (now part of the University of London and known as Birkbeck College).

Jacobs' adult working life began with a clerical position at the Post Office Savings Bank. The job was not a stimulating one but Jacobs put his imagination to good use and started to write short stories, sketches and articles, many of which appeared in the Post Office house publication "Blackfriars Magazine."

Although Jacobs did receive his fair share of rejection slips at the beginning of his career, many works written during this period of clerical employment appeared in the "Idler" and "Today" magazines, both of which were edited by noted humorist Jerome K. Jerome, who had taken a liking to Jacobs' stories.

From 1898, Jacobs also published stories in "The Strand", a popular, monthly fiction and general interest magazine. The arrangement stayed in place for most of his life and many of the works in Jacobs' subsequent collections – including the nautical serialization A Master of Craft (1899-1900) - appeared there first.

Jacobs' first volume of collected works was published in 1896. Many Cargoes, a selection of sea-faring yarns, established Jacobs as a popular writer and humorist with a penchant for authentic dialogue and trick endings (critics of the day referred to him as the "O. Henry of the Waterfront").

A year later he published a novelette, The Skipper's Wooing, and in 1898 and another collection of short stories titled Sea Urchins. These works painted vivid, if imaginatively stretched, pictures of dockland and seafaring London with colourful characters (such as "The Night Watchman", Ginger Dick) that now seem archetypal.

Many of Jacobs' periodical publications and first editions were illustrated with woodcuts and ink drawings, as was still the custom at the turn of the 20th century. The author worked regularly with artists such as E.W. Kemble, who had illustrated Mark Twain's Adventures of Huckleberry Finn and Harriet Beecher Stowe's Uncle Tom's Cabin, and his good friend Will Owen, who eventually became a household name on the strength of his iconic Bisto Kids, Bovril and Lux Soap advertising posters.

By 1899, Jacobs was able to quit the post office and finally begin a career making a living as a full-time writer.

He married the noted suffragist Agnes Eleanor Williams (who had been jailed for her protest activities) in 1900. They set up a household in Loughton, Essex as well as living part of the year in central London. The couple went on to have five children together though their marriage was considered an unhappy one.

The publication of two short novels: At Sunwich Port (a romantic tale of rival sea captains in the fictional seaside community of Sunwich standing in for the actual East England community of Sandwich, Kent) and Dialstone Lane (another small town romance involving intrigue and buried treasure), in 1902 and 1904 respectively, cemented Jacobs' reputation as one of the leading British authors of the new century.

On the foundations of a continuing ability to write for his audience he was readily published though he never strayed too far from what was becoming his familiar, dependable style. There followed a string of further successful publications, including Captain's All (1905), Night Watches (1914), The Castaways (1916), and Sea Whispers (1926). Jacobs published eighteen books in all during his lifetime; thirteen collections and five novels.

As a storyteller, Jacobs is perhaps better remembered for a handful of brief tales of the supernatural than for his popular nautical-themed works. The most famous of these, The Monkey's Paw, originally appeared as part of the 1902 short story collection The Lady of the Barge. It is an economically written story about a shriveled talisman, a monkey's paw that brings grief and horror in the wake of all too literal wish granting. The story has been adapted for other media repeatedly, starting with a one-act play performed at London's Haymarket Theatre in 1903. There have been multiple film adaptations of the story in the modern era; some of us are familiar with its appearance in an episode of the popular animated series, The Simpsons.

Another macabre gem, The Toll-House, was published as part of the collection Sailor's Knots in 1909. Jacob's once again employs a sparse style to tell the story of a group of men who spend the night in a famously haunted house on a dare (a noticeably similar narrative concept was put to use in the much earlier play The Ghost of Jerry Bundler, which had launched Jacobs' parallel career as a dramatist back in 1899 when it was produced at the St. James Theatre in London). Innovative at the time of writing, these sparingly written, atmospheric ghost stories are now familiar classics of the supernatural genre.

Though prolific in his younger years, Jacobs' productivity dropped dramatically after the start of World War I. Yet even in self-imposed semi-retirement Jacobs was still recognized as a leading humorist, ranked alongside such writers as P. G. Wodehouse and George Birmingham. He enjoyed continuing influence and elevated status among his fellow writers as evidenced by these comments attributed to his colleague Henry James:

"Mr. Jacobs, I envy you. You are popular! Your admirable work is appreciated by a wide circle of readers; it has achieved popularity. Mine never goes into a second edition."

James' literary fortunes would, of course, change, but his back-handedly complimentary admiration is compelling evidence of Jacobs' reputation as a writer and humourist both for his audience and his perhaps more admired literary colleagues.

Though Jacobs would create little in the way of new work after 1911, he was still writing. In these later years, seemingly burnt out creatively, Jacobs concentrated more on writing dramatizations and adaptations of his existing stories, including Beauty and the Barge (a film version starring Margaret

Rutherford was also released in 1937) and In the Dark (a one act play that is often performed pr published with The Monkey's Paw adaptation).

Though admired by loyal readers throughout his lifetime, Jacobs has been almost completely forgotten since. Critics are at a loss to name a single reason why - Jacobs is universally considered to be a fine and imaginative literary craftsman. But, as critic John Wain suggested in a 1960 essay, perhaps Jacobs' humour may have been too gentle to persist into the cruel and sarcastic modern era, his dry pokes at proletariat hardship no longer suiting the times.

Nonetheless, Jacobs' legacy remains solid: he continued Dickens' (a writer with whom he is also often compared) tradition for sharing working class stories in authentic vernacular. And polished narratives such as The Monkey's Paw set a standard for the clever use of horror in fiction and popular culture that endures to this day. Indeed recently his works have begun to show an increased demand and appreciation in a world that is constantly looking over its shoulder.

William Wymark Jacobs died in a North London nursing home in Hornsey Lane, Islington on September 1st, 1943, just a week before his 80th birthday.

W.W. Jacobs – A Concise Bibliography

NOVELS AND SHORT STORY COLLECTIONS
MANY CARGOES (SHORT STORIES) (1896)
THE SKIPPER'S WOOING (1897)
SEA URCHINS (SHORT STORIES) (1898) aka MORE CARGOES
A MASTER OF CRAFT (1900)
LIGHT FREIGHTS (SHORT STORIES) (1901)
THE LADY OF THE BARGE (SHORT STORIES) (1902)
AT SUNWICH PORT (1902)
DIALSTONE LANE (1902)
SALTHAVEN (1908)
CAPTAINS ALL (SHORT STORIES) (1911)
NIGHT WATCHERS (SHORT STORIES) (1914)
DEEP WATERS (SHORT STORIES) (1919)

SHORT STORIES (INCLUDING THOSE USED IN THE COLLECTIONS ABOVE)
A BENEFIT PERFORMANCE
A BLACK AFFAIR
A CASE OF DESERTION
A CHANGE OF TREATMENT
A CIRCULAR TOUR
A DISCIPLINARIAN
A DISTANT RELATIVE
A GARDEN PLOT
A GOLDEN VENTURE
A HARBOUR OF REFUGE
A LOVE KNOT
A LOVE PASSAGE
A MARKED MAN

A MIXED PROPOSAL
A RASH EXPERIMENT
A SAFETY MATCH
A SPIRIT OF AVARICE
A TIGER'S SKIN
ADMIRAL PETERS
AFTER THE INQUEST
ALF'S DREAM
AN ADULTERATION ACT
AN ELABORATE ELOPEMENT
AN INTERVENTION
AN ODD FREAK
ANGELS' VISITS
BACK TO BACK
BEDRIDDEN
THE WINTER OFFENSIVE
THE BEQUEST
BILL'S LAPSE
BILL'S PAPER CHASE
BLUNDELL'S IMPROVEMENT
THE BOATSWAIN'S WATCH
THE BOATSWAIN'S MATE
BOB'S REDEMPTION
BREAKING A SPELL
BREVET RANK
BROTHER HUTCHINS
THE BULLY OF THE "CAVENDISH"
THE CABIN PASSENGER
CAPTAIN ROGERS
THE CAPTAIN'S EXPLOIT
CAPTAINS ALL
THE CASTAWAY
THE CHANGELING
"CHOICE SPIRITS"
THE CONSTABLE'S MOVE
CONTRABAND OF WAR
THE CONVERT
THE COOK OF THE "GANNET"
CUPBOARD LOVE
DESERTED
DIRTY WORK
THE DISBURSEMENT SHEET
DIXON'S RETURN
DOUBLE DEALING
THE DREAMER
DUAL CONTROL
EASY MONEY
ESTABLISHING RELATIONS
FAIRY GOLD
FALSE COLOURS
FAMILY CARES

FINE FEATHERS
FOR BETTER OR WORSE
THE FOUR PIGEONS
FRIENDS IN NEED
GOOD INTENTIONS
THE GREY PARROT
THE GUARDIAN ANGEL
THE HEAD OF THE FAMILY
HER UNCLE
HIS LORDSHIP
HIS OTHER SELF
HOMEWARD BOUND
HUSBANDRY
IN BORROWED PLUMES
IN LIMEHOUSE REACH
IN MID-ATLANTIC
IN THE FAMILY
IN THE LIBRARY
JERRY BUNDLER
KEEPING UP APPEARANCES
KEEPING WATCH
THE LADY OF THE BARGE
LAWYER QUINCE
THE LOST SHIP
LOW WATER
MADE TO MEASURE
THE MADNESS OF MR. LISTER
"MANNERS MAKYTH MAN"
MATED
"MATRIMONIAL OPENINGS"
MIXED RELATIONS
MONEY CHANGERS
THE MONEY-BOX
THE MONKEY'S PAW
MRS. BUNKER'S CHAPERON
THE NEST EGG
ODD MAN OUT
THE OLD MAN OF THE SEA
OUTSAILED
OVER THE SIDE
PAYING OFF
THE PERSECUTION OF BOB PRETTY
PETER'S PENCE
PICKLED HERRING
PRIVATE CLOTHES
PRIZE MONEY
THE RESURRECTION OF MR. WIGGETT
THE RIVAL BEAUTIES
RULE OF THREE
SAM'S BOY
SAM'S GHOST

SELF-HELP
SENTENCE DEFERRED
SHAREHOLDERS
SKILLED ASSISTANCE
THE SKIPPER OF THE "OSPREY"
SMOKED SKIPPER
STEPPING BACKWARDS
STRIKING HARD
THE SUBSTITUTE
THE TEMPTATION OF SAMUEL BURGE
THE TEST
THE THREE SISTERS
TO HAVE AND TO HOLD
"THE TOLL-HOUSE"
TWIN SPIRITS
TWO OF A TRADE
THE UNDERSTUDY
THE UNKNOWN
THE VIGIL
WATCH-DOGS
THE WEAKER VESSEL
THE WELL
THE WHITE CAT

STAGE
THE GHOST OF JERRY BUNDLER (1899) (In London)

FILM ADAPTATIONS
A MASTER OF CRAFT (1922)
THE MONKEY'S PAW (1933)
OUR RELATIONS, a Laurel & Hardy film, "suggested by" to Jacobs' "The Money Box." (1936)
FOOTSTEPS IN THE FOG, from the short story The Interruption. (1955)